CODY QUAN
ACT I: BROKEN FAITH

RiceDaddy7 Books

To Mom and Dad
for their unconditioned love.

PREFACE

Cody Quan started out as what psychologists refer to as narrative therapy. I was a lost, unhappy person who one day wanted to write a part of my life down. I wrote with pure emotion resulting in a general disregard for truth. What resulted was a fun house mirror; a deep introspective journey toward all my fears and why I allowed them to control who I am. Warts and all, this was the book I've always wanted to write. It's the proudest thing I've done up to this point. At the very least it answered a question I've always had about how one becomes a writer. The answer, I learned, is that as anything else in life, you choose to become it. When that choice is made, you embrace that journey of enduring the challenges of learning and growing. The same could be said about being Asian-American today. Eastern culture, far more than its Western counterpart, continues to surrender itself to the centuries-old acceptance of parental debt and blind obedience. We aren't the "-American" part of it unless we realize freedom means telling our families to fuck off and owe it to ourselves to choose. At the heart of what this book is about is that simple truth which I found in a complicated way. One day I hope to achieve what Cody achieves, but until then, I will continue putting the pieces together until I am the person that I want to be.

All this being said, not every character in the world of Cody Quan is accurate to their real life counterparts. This is particularly true of the father. On a grander but related scale, not everything in Cody Quan is necessarily reflective of what Asian-America is either. It's impossible to capture such a complicated weave of people into one book. Still, I am a part of that fabric and therefore, my experience lends a small degree of relevancy. Perhaps all I have is one book in me. If that turns out to be the case, I'm still happy to have said some of the most important opinions I have to speak out in the form of fiction. The primary purpose of writing this book was to cleanse me of things that bothered me. Having others read it is a blessed bonus.

- Louis Leung, 2013

CHAPTER 1: BAPTISM

Splash!

The immediate adaptation to cold water from room temperature was intense. After accepting Christ as his savior, Cody Quan had been flung backwards into the baptism pool by the pastor. What followed was shocking to Cody. He had not expected to transcend through time and space. Every prior life event was relived. He felt the soothing comfort of his mother's womb. He felt the pain of falling down from his first bicycle ride. Then came that right hook connecting to Derrick James' face—the day he finally had enough of Derrick's bullying. He saw his first date. Then his first kiss. He recalled all the times in high school when he had snuck out with friends. High school graduation. Art school graduation. College graduation. Thousands of memories flashed through Cody's mind as he experienced a feeling unlike any other.

Finally, Pastor Lu lifted him back up.

The baptism was over. The sounds of the world emerged. It took Cody a while to get used to his senses again. Once he found them, however, the most unexpected thing of all happened. There, standing close to him was Jesus Christ. Jesus was a white guy with the bluest eyes and the sandiest blond hair. He breathed air and had a shadow. Jesus gave Cody the warmest smile he had ever seen.

"You see him now, don't you?" smiled the tubby and jolly Pastor Lu.

"I...I thought it'd just be figurative. You know, God as an invisible force. God as a concept. But...wow," admired Cody.

"Yes, Cody. We see him. Do you still think I'm joking now?" asked his childhood friend Ennis.

Ennis Wong had known Cody since middle school. He immigrated from one of the finest schools in Hong Kong as a teenager, carrying with him a near flawless fluency of the English language. However, Ennis' strong international accent remained. What resulted from his speech patterns was a strange misuse of emphasis on the wrong words. Yet, what stood out about Ennis wasn't where he came from or the unique way in which he spoke—it was the active openness of his Christian faith that defined him. Through persistence and countless personal testimonies, he eventually succeeded in converting Cody as a brother in Christ.

Cody was glad it happened.

Jesus produced an inviting gesture to embrace. As Cody held on to Jesus with tears of joy, he wondered if God's only son spoke English. That's silly, he thought; of course, Jesus spoke English! He's the Creator of all things, right? Now that Cody was a Christian, he stammered for the first thing to say to Christ.

"What's happening, Jesus?!" blurted Cody.

"Okay, okay," chuckled Pastor Lu, ushering Cody away from the podium. "There are a couple more people who can't wait to meet Jesus today too. If you can kindly please get off the stage so that the next person could be baptized..."

Cody apologized and sat back down with his mother. Because she had not been aware of his decision, it was a risk to bring her here. Cody made her promise not to tell his father, a staunch Buddhist. It would break his heart knowing that Cody had accepted Christianity.

Soon after sitting down, Cody felt a tap on his shoulder. It was Luke Lu, the pastor's son and one of Cody's church friends. Cody got up and walked over to him, accepting Luke's handshake as he congratulated Cody on his baptism. Luke had a chiseled, sculptured body. He was tall, handsome, well-built and friendly. Although he was fully Asian, Luke had Caucasian features. Most notable of those Caucasian traits was his Roman-like nose. Many young Asian women in Second Chinese Baptist Church swooned over Luke. He looked like a white guy.

"I love you, Cody," Luke said as he embraced him. "I love you. I love you. I love you."

Luke slowly let go and looked into Cody's eyes. Cody disengaged eye contact, looking at his other church friends who had walked over to congratulate him.

"Cody, you rock, man!" exclaimed Henry Gao.

Henry was one of the few guys who were much shorter than he was. Unlike Cody, though, Henry didn't look very youthful. Although they were of the same age, Henry looked like an old man. He had a whole lot of facial hair and the hairiest arms Cody had ever seen on an Asian man. Henry looked like a smiling troll.

"Congrats!" smiled Marion Yang.

Marion stood in contrast to Henry. She was six-foot-seven, with equal proportions of a normal-looking woman except for her obvious stature. Marion wasn't someone with a lot to say.

"Thanks, Marion," Cody said, stretching his head all the way up. It was like talking to a giraffe.

"Here," Marion beamed, "I brought you a Bible helper book. It has illustrations and quizzes for each part of the New Testament!"

"C.Q.!" shouted a familiar voice next to Cody.

"Felix!" grinned Cody.

"NooooOoOOoo, I wanna hug him first!!!!" intervened a sweet, youthful voice.

The diminutive, spirited body of a beautiful young woman shoved Felix Lin aside, throwing herself onto Cody. Zoey Vu was the prettiest girl in church. She had a reputation of being overly flirty from the way she talked, the provocative way she dressed and her active use of physical touching. Zoey and Felix were the best of friends, almost always being seen together in public.

"I'm so proud of you, baby!" she smiled.

Felix laughed and congratulated him with a handshake. Another person made his way over for congratulations.

"Hey, Cody, congrats. You're still gonna play ball later, right?" asked Jay Zheng.

"Sure, Jay. Definitely," replied Cody.

Cody liked Jay, but he knew so little about him. Physically, Jay was short but wide, standing out at times because of his weight. His friendly personality, however, was also distant. Jay gave the impression that he simply wanted to fit in, avoiding the spotlight whenever he could. In their age group, he was the only other person besides Cody who was a born-again Christian.

"I'll see you then," answered Jay.

As he was shaking Jay's hand, Cody saw a grumpy individual from the corner of his eye. It was Marco Ling, an often unhappy church member who usually seemed angry at one thing or another. Marco had his arms crossed while leaning against a wall. He gave Cody a piercing stare. His thin, round glasses made his beady eyes appear even smaller. Marco had a lot of pimples on his face, validating hushed giggles among the girls that he was the ugliest man in their church.

"Good to see you, Marco," waved Cody.

Marco expectedly didn't respond back, but even his foul temper could not erase what would be one of Cody's happiest days. Cody had taken a chance believing in Jesus, and now he was rewarded in knowing that it was all true. He looked forward to a secure future, one with happiness and assurance.

In the past few years, the popularity of basketball had exploded in the Chinese community. Whether it was in China or anywhere else, almost everyone with a Chinese background, young or old, male or female, was influenced by the shadow of professional basketball player Yao Ming. That shadow was especially strong in the city of Houston where he played for the hometown Rockets. It was only Yao's third season, but to a lot of Chinese-Americans, it seemed like he had played forever. Like a lot of Asian churches during this time, Second Chinese Baptist Church was eager to have its own indoor basketball court. Congregational demand for its construction caused the weekly donation totals to temporarily spike to ten times the usual amount. In under a year, the indoor basketball court was built. It drew the interest of many local men, including the ones not attending the church. The court was beautiful. It had high-quality equipment and was kept clean. It even had its own set of restrooms and locker rooms. For many of the male church members, an afternoon game of hoops was secretly their favorite part of Sunday.

Cody was amongst the young men bouncing one of the many basketballs. It was common for everyone to be joking around, doing warm-ups or practicing shots before the first game. What was uncommon, at least to Cody, was Jesus practicing and conversing with them. Had the Son of God been seen like this every Sunday to the ones who were baptized?

Cody realized he had really missed out.

"Alright, everyone!" announced Felix, "Let's gather around and form teams!"

Forming teams meant everyone standing in line and shooting a free throw. The first person who successfully made a free throw would be on Team A. The second who made it would be on Team B. The third successful person would then go to Team A, and so forth. The alternating pattern would continue until both teams had a total of five players each. If anyone missed, he would simply have to go back in line, awaiting his next turn. Sometimes that second chance never came because the line had so many people. There was a high probability that ten people would have already made a successful free throw by then, establishing the rosters of both teams.

Felix was the first one in line. He took his time, focused on the basket, and succeeded in making the shot. He would be on Team A. Several other players were in line ahead of Cody.

"Hey, man, once again, congrats on the baptism," said Jay, who was in front of him.

"Yeah, it's awesome, man," replied Cody.

While Cody was waiting, he saw his crush, Daphne Lee, making her way through the gym as a shortcut from the rain. Daphne was one of the longtime members of Second Chinese Baptist Church. She was baptized early in life, at the age of five. Cody knew very little about her because he was fairly new.

"Hey, Daphne!" laughed Felix, "Came to enjoy the lovely smell of the court?"

"Shut up!" replied Daphne jokingly.

Even when she was shouting, Daphne's voice was soft and even-keeled, never rising a decibel. Daphne's attire was the same as usual: a conservative long-sleeved sweater and modest pants—complemented with a slight use of makeup. When she was close to passing Cody, she did her best to avoid eye contact. Cody greeted her anyway.

"Hello, Daphne," smiled Cody.

Daphne pretended to look distracted.

"Hey, Daphne," Cody repeated a little louder.

"Oh, uh, hey Cody," she halfheartedly offered, "I heard you got baptized today. Congratulations."

She quickened her pace, nodded toward Jesus, and waited outside in the cold, rainy February weather. However, before the gym doors closed all the way back, Cody saw a car pull over to her. The driver was a handsome, young Caucasian man. He looked a little annoyed with Daphne when she got into his car. The gym door came to a full close, obscuring Cody's view.

"CODY!" shouted Felix.

Cody was snapped back to attention. It was his turn.

"You're going to shoot your free throw or what?" Felix teased.

Cody walked up to the free throw line and dribbled a few times. He then held the ball, squatted up and down, and shot the basketball. The ball went through perfectly without touching the rim. Cody was a good shooter; it was his only strength in the sport. He couldn't play very good defense and he lacked a solid command of his dribbling. He couldn't jump very high and wasn't very fast, and he certainly wasn't tall. But the one thing Cody did better than most was making baskets from long range.

"The Asian Steve Kerr makes it again!" declared Felix.

The free throw shooting continued with the line repeatedly rotating. Everyone besides Felix and Cody missed their shots. Fifteen minutes had passed when Felix lost his patience.

Finally, Felix announced, "Okay, okay, okay. Dang. You guys suck! This isn't working. Seeing how just me and Cody—"

"Cody and I," corrected Henry.

"—pshh. Whatever. Seeing how...Cody and I...are the only two who've made shots, we'll just be the team captains and pick four players each," Felix instructed.

As he said that, two young black men walked in. They were not a part of Second Chinese Baptist Church but, like many others, wanted to play a game of basketball.

"Alright! Some black guys to choose from! I'll take you!" pointed Felix.

The chosen young black man laughed and stood next to Felix.

"Luke!" whispered Marco in protest, "They're black! Do something!"

"They're our brothers in Christ, we should welcome them," Luke replied.

"What?!" whispered Marco.

Marco started shaking with anger.

"Okay, Cody. Your turn. Pick someone," Felix said.

"I pick Jesus!" announced Cody.

"WHAT?!" shouted Marco.

A sudden turn of silence fell upon the basketball court.

"Uh...eh..." The words couldn't come out of Felix's mouth.

"That's the Lord and Savior, you can't just..." Henry couldn't finish his sentence.

"No. It's alright. It's alright. If it is Jesus' will," acknowledged Luke.

Jesus nodded.

"Wait, who are you guys talking to?" asked one of the unbaptized players.

"Jesus. Come to our church sometime and we'll tell you all about Him," smiled Luke.

"Okay, this is a special game where Jesus is playing. Those who aren't baptized, sorry, you're going to have to take a seat because you can't see Jesus," said Felix.

"This is absurd," commented another unbaptized player.

Felix and Cody picked out the rest of their team. Jesus magically adjusted his height to six-foot-seven and altered his clothes from white robes to a set of jersey and shorts. The jersey featured the word "Christ" on the back. His jersey number was "1." Cody was super excited about the game. Playing basketball with the Creator of the universe was far more incredible than even playing with Michael Jordan.

"Okay, just to be clear, here are the rules like always," said Felix. "Whichever team that gets to twenty-one points first is the winner. Each made basket counts as one point. Each basket made from behind the three-point line will be counted as two points."

"Duece?" asked one of the players.

"No deuce. Straight up twenty-one points," answered Felix.

When the game began, the mismatch between both teams became evident. Jesus Christ was unstoppable. He did windmill dunks from the

free throw line. He blocked every shot by the opposing team. His passes were always perfect. Those on the sidelines who weren't playing saw different versions. For the baptized, they saw Jesus performing miracles on the basketball court. The others, however, saw Cody performing dunks and other illogical actions. All were flabbergasted.

Cody's team eventually won by a final score of twenty-one to zero. As the players lined up at the water fountain, Ennis took Cody aside.

"Hey, don't do that anymore. Serious. Don't," he warned.

"Why not?" asked Cody.

"Because he's God," explained Ennis. "You can't just request and pray for anything. What will you do next, huh? Ask him to get you a nice car? A pretty girl? Don't be so selfish! He is our Lord!"

"He didn't seem to have a problem with it," laughed Cody.

"Tsk. You just don't get it, do you? I'll pray for you,"

promised Ennis.

Cody shrugged and sipped from the water fountain. When he was finished, he went around looking for Jesus.

"Hey, have you seen Jesus?" Cody asked Henry. "Where'd he go?"

Henry shrugged.

"Have you seen Jesus?" he asked another player. "What about you? Anyone?"

Cody finally came to the conclusion that Jesus had left. Perhaps he had a starving kid to save? Maybe there was a bus about to crash? But couldn't Jesus be everywhere at once? asked Cody to himself. Were there multiple Jesuses?

There were so many questions.

———

Pastor Lu quietly looked out the window as he sat in his chair. The heavy storm that started an hour after service stubbornly remained into the late afternoon. It made it seem like nighttime. The pastor's office was small but well-furnished. The extreme tidiness served as evidence of his attention toward detail and responsibility. Although he was in his late fifties, memories from where he had come from were still fresh in his mind. He remembered growing up in Shanghai while it was being rebuilt. The city had recovered fairly quickly during China's Cultural Revolution, but not fast enough for a man like Wai Li Lu. Lu was interested in the steady quality of education that the United States had to offer. So, like many of his generation during the seventies, he tried to immigrate westward to the other side of the world. Due to an uncle using bribery, Lu's citizenship was approved and he moved to New York City. He was a skinny man back then. However, not long after he arrived, he experienced a tremendous weight gain. Lu interpreted it as a symbol of happier times and opportunities.

From that point on, his story became a boring one. Wai

Li Lu studied hard, obeyed his parents, courted the recommended girl from his congregation, married her and then got an accounting job with a Houston gas company. Houston was the city where his son Luke was born. Once he was away from the comfortable surroundings of New York's Chinatown, Wai Li Lu assimilated as Willy Lu. "Please," he would good-naturedly insist to his American coworkers, "Just call me Willy." He saw the Texas oil boom during the eighties as a sign from God. He prospered and moved his family into a good neighborhood. His house was in a recent development in the then obscure city of Sugar Land, Texas. Although Sugar Land was technically its own city, it was considered by everyone to be a part of the greater Houston area. Willy Lu would have remained at his job for the rest of his life, but the industry fell apart from the domino effect of the Enron scandal.

Once again, Willy Lu saw it as another sign from God. He felt a calling to train in a seminary and became part of a big church in the Houston Chinese community. His ascension as a pastor controversially came after the original church had split. There, he took as many ex-members of its congregation as he could, starting a new church.

That was how he became Pastor Lu.

"<This man. This...preacher. I'm not so sure>," opined a member of his staff, Reverend Han, in their native Mandarin Chinese language.

"<This church won't grow fast enough like this. Our members aren't the most evangelistic type, just look at our annual baptism today. That was only five people, two of them were teenagers.>" Pastor Lu paused to take off his glasses. "<I have prayed many nights ...>"

"<I'm sure you have>," interrupted Reverend Han, "<but we are a Chinese church. We are suddenly letting all these...these black people in. Lu, this preacher is not one of us. Our methods may differ.>"

Reverend Han handed back the prospective preacher's resume. Pastor Lu looked at it again. Paper-clipped to the resume was a photo of the recently ordained preacher, a round and youthful black man in his early forties with a smile even jollier than Lu's.

The resume was written by hand.

"<He has beautiful handwriting. And he insists he can bring in fifty regular members from his former congregation. We have around seventy-seven or seventy-eight people. This would almost double our Sundays. Imagine, a morning service with an audience of over a hundred. Doubling the...>" Pastor Lu stopped himself because he was about to mention the obvious increase in donations.

In his heart, he didn't want to think he did his job as a pastor for money, because it wasn't about money for him. The church is new, he thought, justifying all the extra finances the church could spend. Besides, he thought, his anniversary with his wife was coming up in just under two months...it would be nice to get her something special for once.

The other reverend began to speak.

"<All fifty of this new preacher's members are African-American. I've been invited to a couple of their services. They worship very differently. Our conservative Chinese members would be scared off. What would we do if they started leaving and just the black ones are left? I am not going to dance and shake myself. I...I would leave, Lu>," said Reverend Ping.

Pastor Lu silently looked at his desk. In public, he was jolly and charismatic. In the confines of his close friends and congregation, however, he revealed himself to be a man of fierce determination.

"<If we must join with another non-Chinese pastor, couldn't we at least get a white one or what about a Vietnamese one? There are plenty of Vietnamese churches in Houston>," suggested Reverend Han.

"<Yes>," smiled Reverend Ping, "<a white congregation would be good!>"

"<I tried. There was little interest. And Vietnamese people are usually Catholic. I even asked the new Korean preachers. Nothing. The Bible says we are all brothers and sisters. This new preacher is our Christian brother.
Now, I...I haven't seen, nor heard, from our Lord in years. But I still feel Him. I believe we get to a certain point where the Lord communicates us with suggestive signs. He reads our hearts as

well as our minds. Seeing, I suppose, is for the weaker faith.
The stronger ones, like us, we transcend
this. That's what I've come to understand, anyway. Brother Han,
Brother Ping...I'm certain this is what Jesus wants>," said
Pastor Lu. "<I'm certain of it.>"

"<Well, have you at least talked with some other
members of the church?>" asked Reverend Han.

Pastor Lu had no answer.

"<They may not be pleased>," Han continued. "<We
assured them that this would be a Chinese-only church.>"

Pastor Lu wiped sweat from the corner of his forehead,
"<I'm their pastor, am I not? Since when haven't I made
decisions that were for the good of our church? I pray for those
decisions. I have made my decision, my brothers. First thing
I'm going to do tomorrow is have lunch with this preacher. If
everything goes well, I will make him co-pastor. Second
Chinese Baptist Church will be renamed to Fellowship
Communion Baptist Church. Final decision.>"

The lack of democracy created an air of pause in the
room.

"<Reverend Han. Lead us to prayer.>"

"<Of course>," Reverend Han replied.

The two reverends and the pastor held hands as
Reverend Han recited a long prayer. The old reverend prayed
for guidance, understanding and a brighter future for both the
church and its individual members. Pastor Lu's eyes slightly
opened during the prayer. He closed them again, envisioning
the brand new Mercedes that he had always wanted.

———

February weather in Houston is unpredictable. Even
within hours on the same day, the temperature sinks to freezing
cold from burning hot. Other days, like this particular Sunday, a

cloudless morning can transform into an afternoon of ceaseless rain. Before his baptism, Cody would have explained it as precipitation. Now, he defined it as the work of Jesus Christ.

It was now six o'clock and the basketball court had closed for the day. Cody stood outside of it, waiting for the storm to pass. Everyone else had lost patience, fleeing to their cars amid the punishing rain. Poor Henry discovered his car's remote was broken when he reached his little Hyundai Sonata. Marco slipped into a deceptively deep puddle of muddy water. He was so angry he grabbed the person running next to him and forced him into the puddle too. Ennis got soaked running all over the lot, realizing that he had forgotten where he parked. By the time he found his car, Ennis was a total mess. He looked like he had come out of a swimming pool. Luke and Felix, sharing an umbrella, walked across the parking lot and got into Luke's car and waited for the rain to stop. Now there are some people with common sense, thought Cody.

Meanwhile, many questions about Jesus swirled inside of Cody's head. Why did Jesus disappear after the first basketball game? How come some of the baptized couldn't see Jesus? Did Jesus want to be called Jesus? Maybe Mr. Christ, or more likely, Lord and Heavenly Father? It was like logic had flipped upside down for Cody. Nothing made sense. Does he go through life now pretending that things are still the same? Or should he quit his job and tell everyone what he had seen, like Paul from the Bible?

"So many questions," uttered Cody out loud.

Then, something caught his eye.

Someone was moving behind one of the pillars. Because the lighting was poor and the weather conditions were less than ideal, Cody's sight was limited. Determined to find an answer, he squinted his eyes, hoping to improve his vision.

"Jesus?" called out Cody. "Is that you?"

The silhouette came closer to a slightly more lit area. It was enough light for Cody to realize that it really was Jesus. He was now dressed in ragged clothes, far different from the shiny basketball outfit he had worn earlier. More importantly was Jesus' change in expression. Gone was the friendly, inviting smile. In its place was an angry, hateful look. Cody remained still, like a deer in headlights.

"Jesus...Lord...Heavenly Father...why are you looking at me like that?!" Cody asked.

The eerie figure of Jesus silently and slowly walked closer to Cody. He felt spooked now. Jesus finally approached to within a few feet away from Cody and then stopped. Cody blurted out the first question he had wanted to ask.

"Why? Why is there so much pain and suffering in this world when you could just stop it?" he inquired.

Jesus looked at him silently.

"Why are people born only to die?" Cody asked, feeling bolder.

No answer came out of Christ's lips.

"What's the point of heaven and hell if people don't even know you exist?"

Finally, Cody found the courage to ask his most daring question.

"DO YOU EVEN CARE?" he shouted.

And like a tiger, Jesus pounced on Cody and violently punched him until Cody lay shocked and stunned on the ground. What happened? he wondered. He felt Jesus breathe close to his ear.

"Fuck. You," the Messiah replied.

And then Jesus was gone, leaving Cody alone in a bloody pulp.

CHAPTER 2: TIME WAITS FOR NO ONE

If there were one particular word to describe the root of Cody's problems, it would be this: punctuality. It was a concept that he struggled to understand. Perhaps it was a reflection of self-centeredness or the result of being a perfectionist. Neither of these or other reasons, however, interested his supervisor, Rachel Hutchens. To her, Cody was consistently late.

What wasn't so much of a mystery was how Cody kept getting away with it. He was part of a new breed of designers, ones who were as adept in art as they were at programming. Cody's skill set made him the prince of his castle; that castle's name was the University of Houston. There, he was working with soon-to-be senior citizens, pushing past their fifties. To many of them, Cody's talent was a gem. It was Rachel who initially saw Cody's outstanding resume and capabilities. Although he had originally applied for the wrong position, she begged her boss to create a new one for Cody.

It proved to be a big mistake for Rachel.

Her boss and others in their department fell in love with Cody's abilities. They spoiled him by letting him bend rules. He became a nightmare employee for a supervisor like Rachel. Cody's favorite bad habit was intentional tardiness. He deliberately came to work two hours later than he was scheduled. This was done in front of Rachel's face. It made her look powerless and disrespected. It was the same song and dance every time. Cody would come in late, Rachel would ask him why and then Cody would shrug it off.

This particular Monday morning, however, drew

Rachel's ire more than usual. As soon as Cody came in, she shot from her desk and walked toward his. Rachel's anger was apparent when she pulled a chair next to him and sat on it with resounding authority.

"You're two hours late. Again. Like you are everyday," she seethed.

"I'm, uh, heh, sorry?" Cody smirked.

"You're sorry? You're sor—. Ugh! You're going down, Cody. Someday, somehow, I'll find a way to bring you down. You are so lucky to be doing what you're doing. Did you know what I did when I was your age? I was a fucking gym teacher. I came to work on time every day. I made something close to minimum wage. And you're trying to convince me that you're 'sorry?' If it was up to me, you'd have already been fired! You're lucky people higher up than me like you, Cody Quan. But you aren't shit to me. You're not!" Rachel's head was about to explode.

"I'm sorry, Rachel. But I always leave two hours after everyone else. It's still eight hours of work that I put in," justified Cody.

"I don't give a rat's ass!" Rachel replied. "You can't just make new rules here! What does that make me? I look like a chump!"

Cody knew what he had done was wrong, but somehow he found it difficult to be punctual. He was never punctual for anything. Not school, not work, not even for his own birth; he was born weeks after his expected due date. Most people who knew him often joked that he'd probably be late for his own funeral. Sometimes his extreme tardiness was humorous. Most times, however, it wasn't. It shocked Rachel that Cody had often gotten away with being late without consequence. He was either incredibly lucky or exceptionally special.

"You missed training the new intern this morning," hissed Rachel.

"Damn," commented Cody, "I'm sorry for that too."

"Stop saying you're sorry, Cody! Because you're not." She paused to calm down. "She's still here. Now be more professional and show her around."

Rachel stood up and went back to her desk.

Moments later, the intern made her way to Cody's cubicle. She was deliberately distant. She sat around quietly, making little eye contact while tightly clutching her belongings. For the first thirty minutes, Cody saw more of her back than her face. He eventually learned that her name was Mindy Cheung.

"So...Mindy, is it?...You're transferred from the optometry department, eh?" asked Cody.

"Yes," Mindy hastily replied. She was fidgeting with the Internet cables of her laptop.

Cody waited for her to follow up on her reply, but soon realized that it was the full extent of their conversation. Slowly, he turned back around to his workstation. Cody skimmed through the clutter of work-related emails. He was hoping for a reply back to a flirtatious lunch invitation he had written to Daphne, his crush from Second Chinese Baptist Church. She often didn't reply back. When she did, however, they were direct and formal answers without a hint of romantic interest.

He decided to write another email:

"Hey babe, how's your body stopping traffic today? Don't break too many hearts. Would like to know if you'd like to have lunch with me this week. It's not often I get to have lunch with a goddess. Let's make it a habit. Looked hot at church yesterday. - X's, O's and Cheerios, Cody Q."

Cody clicked on the Send icon, casting another line of bait into the cyberspace waters.

"Need any help?" he asked the new intern.

"No," Mindy replied.

She placed her purse between them, creating a barricade. Cody excused himself to go to the restroom. It was a ploy he often used to get out of the building. During the peak hours, the University of Houston was like its own city. Thousands upon thousands of students walked onto its numerous labyrinths of pathways. Previously, Cody had dated one of the students here, but realized someone in his late twenties did not have much in common with girls in their late teens. The school was diverse, but he felt lonely. It was made up of mostly people in their late teens or aged forty and above. Perhaps I've been here too long, thought Cody.

Whenever he wanted to be alone, Cody would walk to one of his favorite places on campus—the old Roy Cullen building. It was musty and relatively ancient, dating back to the late 1930s. The top floor, which was rumored to be haunted, was damp and dark. Because of this, Cody found it to be a great place for solitude. It was the first place he had in mind to collect his thoughts about what had happened at his baptism yesterday.

He was very confused as to why Jesus was friendly enough to play basketball with him, but then would later violently beat him. It was as though Christ was bipolar. More strangely, Cody immediately healed, showing no signs of injury.

"Dear Heavenly Father," he closed his eyes and prayed. "Hallowed is your name. I was wondering if you could, you know, show yourself."

Moments of silence followed. Cody tried again.

"Dear God...Jesus...I need to talk. If you don't mind," he prayed.

He looked around expecting Jesus to be there, but there was nothing. Were the events from yesterday a hallucination? They couldn't be, thought Cody, others saw Jesus too.

Disappointed, Cody headed back.

In his cubicle, he found Mindy doing tutorials for the Adobe Photoshop software. She was noticeably struggling, but her pride prevented her from soliciting help from Cody. In Mindy's mind, he was Asian-American, which meant he probably looked down on her. As a native from Taiwan, she wished there was another Taiwanese worker around to converse with. Instead, Cody was the only Asian in their department, but he was like a banana—yellow on the outside, white on the inside. Mindy took notice that the department was purposely diversified with people of different races, gender and handicap. Clearly affirmative action in place, she thought to herself. She eyed the Americans suspiciously.

"Hey, you're doing it wrong," a voice interrupted her

train of thought.

It was Cody. He had been looking at her laptop screen from where he was sitting.

"Um. O-Okay," Mindy muttered, "What am I doing wrong?"

Mindy pretended to fidget with the software, hoping Cody would divert his attention elsewhere. After a minute of acting, she looked back up. Cody was still looking at her, but now he was also eating a box of Pocky.

"You're trying to make a reflection, right? Use the gradient tool for your mask," munched Cody.

"B-but the book says..."

"Here, let me show you..." he insisted.

Cody reached over and did the whole tutorial in a few seconds. While he was doing it, his fingers worked in a blurred motion.

"Wow!" she smiled in admiration.

Cody went back to his computer and started checking his emails. Still no reply from Daphne, he said to himself. Frustrated, he fidgeted around his desk. He yearned for a window. Every other cubicle was located near a window that featured a view of the giant fountain in the middle of campus. Perhaps Rachel did this deliberately? I guess she has subtle ways of getting back at me, thought Cody.

"Hey, hey!" Mindy shook Cody's shoulder.

She was suddenly very close to him.

"Yeah?" he answered.

"You speak Chinese?"

"No."

"Why not? Don't your parents teach you?"

"I speak decent Cantonese. Does that work?"

"You should learn. It's the most important language," she explained.

A sudden burst of energy gave Mindy an animated behavior.

"Hey! Teach me how to double her!" she demanded.

"What? 'Double her?'"

"The picture! Audrey Hepburn! She's my favorite. I'm just trying to learn this other tutorial. Ms. Rachel made me," said Mindy. "Double her picture for me. I need to show Ms. Rachel. Then I get to go home."

Cody began cloning the digitally cutout photo of Audrey Hepburn. Like an art director, Mindy gave directions on how she wanted the canvas to be decorated.

"Okay...move the tree there. Make the background pink...add a sun...no, a moon is better...can you use a different font?...make it glow..." she instructed.

The final result was amateurish, which made it that more believable that Mindy had done it. She sent it as an attachment to Rachel and started packing up to leave.

"Thanks so much!" Mindy smiled with glee. "Tomorrow, you will do my other tutorials for me! Goodbye!"

"Wait, what...?" asked Cody.

———————

Duke wasn't the chosen one.

That distinction belonged to his cousin Cody, who was the last male heir of their family. Cody was an only child, whose father was the only son among his grandfather's six children. In Chinese culture, males who carry the family name are more beloved. Duke would've given anything to be a Quan. Instead, because this was his mother's side of the family, Duke was a Feng.

"Grandma, it's me, Duke," he announced in a solemn voice.

The one the family called Skinny Grandma opened her eyes. It was the first time she had smiled since her stay at the hospital. She was lucky. The city of Houston is well-known for its medical center, comprising the best collection of hospitals and medical staff the world has to offer. Because many billionaires and their family members had been saved there, generous donations were often given to the medical center. This made the hospitals seem more like five-star hotels. It was well understood that if someone couldn't be saved at the medical center, funeral services should be in order. Skinny Grandma had been diagnosed with a heart condition. The doctors attributed it to thinning heart vessels, which increased her risk of a stroke.

Duke had brought her congee and egg tarts from Houston's Chinatown. Because he lived in Dallas, he was a bit drained from the long four-hour drive. Yet, nothing was more important to him than being there for the grandmother who raised him and Cody. Duke was a very serious person. His de facto expression was comprised of a frown and an arrogant stare. His posture was as austere as it was stringent.

"Hi there," greeted the heart surgeon, "I was told you were already informed of the specifics of the procedure. The risk is high. She has a lot of blockage. We've tried to do it without surgery, but now it looks like it might come down to that."

The doctor went on to explain the procedure in detail to Duke. Once he finished, he took his leave. Moments later, footsteps could be heard running toward the room. It was Cody.

"Granndddmmaaa!" he smiled.

She laughed while being hugged by Cody. Duke's expression remained unchanged, with only a mere movement of his eyebrow hinting of his disapproval. To him, Cody appeared like a child.

"<My favorite grandson! Turn around and let me spank you!>" requested Skinny Grandma.

Cody turned around while his grandmother playfully spanked him.

"<Spank!>" she laughed.

"Hey, Duke, thanks for making it," said Cody.

Duke shrugged.

"At least one of us cared enough to show up on time. Now she can begin her operation as scheduled. I filled out all the paperwork," Duke said. "Things you should have done but you never do. Because you're a child and you're spoiled. You don't deserve this woman's love."

"Go to hell," remarked Cody.

Duke shrugged.

"<Why do you boys speak so much English in front of your dear old grandmother? I thought I raised you both better than that. Don't forget all of your Chinese, Cody>," requested Skinny Grandma.

"<Yes, Cody. Don't forget all your Chinese, white boy>," Duke sneered.

"<Laugh don't me dare beat for to>," Cody attempted in broken Cantonese.

"<Ai-ya, Cody! It seems that you've forgotten all of your Chinese! You need to get yourself a nice girlfriend from China, so that she can speak Chinese to you all day long. This way, you wouldn't forget>," she advised.

"Heh. A girlfriend. That'll be a long time coming," laughed Duke.

"<And what about you, Gay Wind? What happened to your girlfriend?>" Skinny Grandma asked Duke, using his Chinese name.

Cody chuckled, "Gay Wind."

Duke did not find the verbal jab at his name humorous. He chose to ignore Cody instead.

"<My previous girlfriend. She was...not very virtuous>," Duke explained.

"<I have told you to watch out for those Taiwanese girls, haven't I? Get yourself a nice Chinese girl too, Gay Wind>," she said.

Skinny Grandma paused to collect her thoughts. Cody and Duke knew she was about to delve into a more serious matter.

"<Min-Guang, Gay Wind>," she called both of them in their Chinese names. "<If your dear grandmother doesn't make it after this operation, just know that I'm okay with it. It could be my time. Everybody has to go someday. If this is my last moment, seeing you both have made me a very happy woman. I would only regret not seeing either of you marry and have grandchildren.>"

"<Time it is not your>," said Cody.

Even though his Chinese was awful, Skinny Grandma knew what he was trying to say.

"<You're such a shoe shine boy, Min-Guang>," his

grandmother smiled.

In China, a shoe shine boy was someone who knew how to sweet-talk. The heart surgeon entered the room again, this time with three assistants.

"Okay, guys," he began, "We've got to prep her for her operation tonight. We'd appreciate it if y'all wait outside."

Both cousins walked out of the hospital room. Their body language and distant personal space reflected a long-held animosity towards one another. Neither wanted to leave Skinny Grandma right away.

"You're still gonna stay here?" Cody asked.

"Someone has to," muttered Duke.

"No, no one has to. Methodist is a good hospital. This is a professional facility. One of the best in the world. They can take care of her without your meddling," Cody said.

"Then you can go on with your life and be selfish like you always have," dismissed his cousin.

Cody and Duke stared each other down. Duke had mastered the lion's stare, never backing off from a challenge, real or perceived. He was much bigger in stature than Cody, which helped him intimidate his cousin. Eventually, Cody stared away and directed his attention elsewhere.

"So," Cody broke the silence,"still doing auditing?"

"Yes," Duke replied, giving him a minimal answer.

"What about your dating coach seminars? Still doing those?" asked Cody.

Duke had been holding a series of seminars that focused on the empowerment of Asian men in dating opportunities. His philosophy was to create the identity of the alpha male. It was a state of mind set on establishing a superior position on the totem pole of race dating in America.

"I'm not a 'dating coach.' I hold seminars for empowerment. I save lives. You need to come. You need my help," Duke assured.

Cody paused for a moment.

"Okay. How about this? I'll go to one of your silly seminars if you come to one of our church retreats," offered Cody.

"I'll gain nothing," calculated Duke, "while you'll gain

everything."

"What do you mean by that? No one but loser guys attend your seminars. There are actually cute girls in our church retreats. I'm the one with nothing to gain. You get girls and the word of Jesus whom, by the way, I met yesterday," exclaimed Cody.

"You...'met'...Jesus?" laughed Duke.

"Yeah!" smiled Cody.

"Why do you always lie, Cody?" responded Duke. "Lying is a trait of the beta male. You are using a detoured passive-aggressive stance to achieve your goal. This is the kind of habit I wish to remove from you and other weak men. As Asian men, we need to take back what's —"

"Hey, look, it's Pete Mok!" interrupted Cody.

He had spotted their childhood friend Pete from across the hospital floor. Pete, Duke and Cody were once very close. The years had not been kind for the high school dropout. Pete had fallen into the drug-dealing life, resulting in imprisonment for most of his early twenties. Neither cousin had seen him for awhile, but they heard the rumors about what had happened to him. The current incarnation of Pete resembled very little the goofy kid with the heart of gold they once had known. Yet, Cody knew that underneath Pete's tattoos and baggy pants, he was that same person.

"Pete!" shouted Cody from across the hall.

Pete looked around, trying to make sense of his reality. He had a look of disorientation and confusion, which was a result of the daily drugs that he was taking.

"Pete!" Cody continued waving. "Dude, it's me, Cody!"

"Oh whadda C, wha up nigga, been awhile ain't none done," Pete cryptically replied.

Pete gave Cody a unique high five that he had developed from the streets. He attempted to do the same with Duke, but Duke simply greeted Pete with a smileless nod.

"What are you doing here, man? It's been years," asked Cody.

"Ah, you know how it be, nigga. Some nigga clipped my girl's ma tryin' a mug it up in C. Town and we handlin' bizness. What up wit' you, my childhood nigz?" Pete sniffed in between his sentences, an obvious sign of active cocaine use.

"I found Jesus, man," Cody answered with conviction.

"Ah, for real? Dang, nigga. I need sum of dat myself." Pete tapped Duke on the forearm. "My man, ain't seen you since ninety-eight back in the S.W.A.T. Look at choo, bitch azz got married yet? Say, I need a cig break. Y'all wanna cut loose?"

"No, man, we're good. So what have you been up to, Pete?" asked Cody.

Pete raised his voice, "Maaaannn I—"

"Big P.! Tuan is on the phone!" interrupted one of his friends from across the hall. "He madder dan a motherfuck, nigga."

Forgetting to say his goodbyes, Pete rushed back toward the other end of the hospital floor hallway.

Duke shook his head with judgment and a hint of disgust.

"He's going to be dead before he hits thirty," he estimated.

Cody walked toward the elevators. He didn't wanted to be there with Duke longer than he had to. His cousin was uncomfortable to be around. In fact, thought Cody, if he weren't related to me, I wouldn't even be talking to him. He had always felt a bit of danger around Duke, who had a hyper-competitive streak. It was a result of Duke's superiority complex.

While waiting for the elevator, Cody took one final look at the surroundings. On one end of the floor was Duke, standing next to their grandmother's room. He was deep in thought, perhaps bearing the weight of responsibility. On the other end was Big Pete and his entourage, tending to a fallen ally. They were joking and happy. There was a touch of carpe diem about them with a clear disregard for consequence. Both Duke and Pete possessed opposing schools of thought. Was his cousin right to stay responsible at the expense of contentment? Or was it better to be someone like Pete, who was happy and cared so little about the future? These were the thoughts racing through Cody's mind as he waited for the elevator to come.

———————

Houston would not be confused as an extraordinarily beautiful American city. It lacks the majestic mountains and palm trees of Los Angeles. It is devoid of an endless adornment of monolithic skyscrapers like Manhattan. There is a perceived lack of popular history, unlike that of other major American cities such as Chicago, Boston, San Francisco, Seattle or Philadelphia. Above all, it lacks the perception for fun like Miami or Las Vegas. All these viewpoints, however, failed to illustrate what so many Houstonians felt about their city: It would one day be the future of America.

As he made his way across different parts of town, Cody saw glimpses of what would someday be. He drove past the rudimentary monorail that was in its beginning stages of citywide public transportation. He passed by the beautiful lofts that drew the migration of carpetbaggers. The city was constantly bright with electricity, illuminating new ventures and construction projects.

Houston, locals predicted, would be a force to be reckoned with.

Cody loved driving on the city's freeways during the evenings. Catch a perfect winter night and the temperature is ideal, he thought. The drive from the medical center area to his house was approximately twenty minutes. He deliberately took thirty. Relatively speaking, Cody had done well for himself. At the age of twenty-five, he had bought his own place, a beautiful three-story townhouse in a popular part of town. He lived on the strip of Westheimer Road near the Piney Point area. Like most Asian-American men of his generation, Cody had a well-paying job, excellent financial security and medical benefits. Yet, also like most Asian-American men his age, he was prone to spend as much as he made. There was a feeling of financial invincibility, giving him the illusion that he could live above his means.

Cody made his way towards the closed gate of his complex. He stopped right before it to type in his four-digit password. When he couldn't reach the panel, he cursed his shortness and got out of his car to manually enter the numbers in. When the gate finally opened, Cody got back into his car and drove on through. He cranked up the volume of his stereo, navigating his way through the twists and turns of his neighborhood. He was seconds away from home, sweet home.

Then, he noticed a familiar scene which triggered his temper.

"Oh, no. No...NO!" he shouted.

The lights inside Cody's three-story townhouse had been turned on. Through the blinds of the second floor he could make out a silhouette moving around. That person was digging through his belongings. He recognized the figure right away. It was his father. Cody angrily stormed inside, rushing upstairs to the second floor.

"<There you are!>" smiled his father. "<We were wondering when you'd return. Why didn't you answer your phone?>"

Kelvin Min-Lo Quan was a happy, easygoing man. He was well-liked. Cody resembled him in looks, but unlike his father, he was prone to hotheadedness.

"WHY ARE YOU GUYS DOING THIS?! GET THE FUCK OUT OF THIS HOUSE! NOW!!!" Cody screamed in English.

He scanned the second floor where his kitchen and living room were. Food was scattered everywhere. His Playstation 2 was being used as a DVD player on full blast for a Cantonese movie. The stairs leading to the floor above were littered with tied-up grocery bags recycled as trash bags. Cody pushed his father aside and stormed upstairs to the third floor. He wanted to speak with the mastermind behind this latest home invasion.

Finally, Cody located the culprit based on the loud sounds of the washer and dryer along with the running water from the bathtub. There, he confronted his mother. She was rearranging his clothes, sorting out the ones she approved or disapproved of.

"LEAVE THIS HOUSE N—" Cody began in English.

"<HOW MUCH DID THIS NEW SHIRT COST?!!!>"

his mother screamed back. "<AND THIS ONE! THIS IS BANANA REPUBLIC! BANANA REPUBLIC IS EXPENSIVE! IT'S AT LEAST FIFTY DOLLARS! WHY DO YOU WASTE SO MUCH MONEY?>"

"I JUST WASHED THAT BANANA REPUBLIC SHIRT! WHY ARE YOU WASHING IT AGAIN?"

Marie Wong was very tiny in stature but possessed a booming presence. She had stayed at four-foot-nine since she was twelve. However, growing up as the second eldest sister of eight siblings had molded her into a naturally domineering person. She was used to looking up at people and wagging her finger at them. Very little intimidated her. Cody, however, was the exception.

"<GIVE ME YOUR WALLET!>" she ordered in Cantonese.

When Cody hesitated, she reached into his left pocket, pulling the wallet out herself. She knew Cody never had much cash in it. She also knew that if there were cash, he would spend it instead of using his credit and debit cards. Cody's mother got her purse and started putting money into his wallet.

"<I gave you thirty-five dollars last weekend and now there's only two dollars left. What did you use the money for?>" she inquired.

Cody was growing very annoyed that she was trying to control every aspect of his life.

"<I ate with it>," answered Cody.

"<That was just two days ago! You spent that much money? I cooked for you! I left you enough food for both lunch and dinner. Why are you eating out, huh?!!!>"

"<'CAUSE I'M SICK AND TIRED OF YOUR COOKING! I WANNA EAT WHAT I WANNA EAT!>"

"<I'M JUST TRYING TO SAVE YOU MONEY! MY COOKING IS HEALTHIER THAN AMERICAN RESTAURANT FOOD!>"

"YEAH, RIGHT!" Cody screamed. "THIS IS ALL ABOUT CONTROL LIKE IT ALWAYS IS! JUST LIKE THE OTHER DAY WHEN I BOUGHT GROCERIES TO COOK AND YOU JUST CAME IN AND TOOK EVERYTHING BACK TO YOUR HOUSE! YOU DON'T

LIKE IT WHEN I COOK, YOU DON'T LIKE IT WHEN I
IRON AND WASH MY OWN CLOTHES, YOU DON'T
LIKE IT WHEN—>"

"<Hey, hey, hey! Both of you calm down!!!>" shouted
Cody's father after he had come up from the second
floor. "<Please stop fighting! We've got to have peace!>"

"<QUAN MIN-LO!>" she ordered her husband,
"<GET YOUR ASS BACK DOWNSTAIRS AND WATCH
TELEVISION!"

"<I just...I just want you both to stop fighting!>"
pleaded Mr. Quan.

"<ARE YOU SIDING AGAINST ME? ARE YOU?>"
she looked at him, daring him to challenge her.

"<No...I...I'm going back downstairs>," he complied.

The loss of control was too much for Cody to bear.
Externally, he resembled his father. Cody had dark olive skin, a
similar speech pattern, expressive creativity and a laugh like his
dad. But there was much of Cody that resembled his mother,
particularly her temper. Cody and his mother were like oil and
water. Once Cody reached a maximum boiling point, he did not
react verbally—he reacted violently.

"AHHHHHHHHHHHHHHHH!!!!!!!!" Cody let out a
primal scream.

He then punched a hole into his bathroom wall.
WHAM!

The cheap flimsy plaster made it seem like Cody had
super strength. The hole was large, ugly and a sign of more
destruction to come.

"<Stop, son, stop! No, no, no!>" his father begged.

Cody repeatedly punched his closet door, smashing it
past recognition. He grabbed toothbrushes and deodorant
bottles, tossing them randomly throughout the bathroom. He
kicked the toilet until his foot started hurting. Cody's mother
burst into tears and grabbed her son. Cody flung her to the
floor, using what self-control he had left to stop from
kicking her. Instead, he started stomping on the tile floor.

"YOU WANT A PIECE OF ME?! YOU WANT TO
CONTROL MY LIFE?!!" screamed Cody.

The voice coming out of him was from something else.

He sounded like a monster.

"<Please...please...stop!>" His mother grabbed Cody's clothes and wallet.

He grabbed the wallet back and threw it across the room. He followed up with his clothes and did the same.

"NO! I DON'T WANT YOU TO WASH MY CLOTHES! I DON'T WANT YOU TO GIVE ME MONEY!" yelled Cody.

Mr. Quan held his sobbing wife, hoping the sudden silence would cool things down. Fights between Cody and his mother were commonplace. Cody breathed heavily, allowing his heart rate to return back to normal. He had come close to hitting his mother in every fight, but the closest he had come to it was when he pushed her down tonight. It was only a matter of time, he concluded, that he would snap and brutally attack her.

It was the consequence of culture.

When she was growing up in Hong Kong, boys weren't considered men until they were married. Their mothers were expected to coddle them. Then this practice was transferred over to their wives, who spoiled them. Women of her generation were a symbol of power and pride. While American culture's belief that a woman's place in the kitchen was considered sexist, Chinese women of his mother's generation saw it as a forum for control and empowerment. Cody, meanwhile, saw the whole process as emasculating. How could he expect to compete against other men for women? He had parents who were trying to make him as ignorant of basic life skills as possible. They didn't want him to know how to iron, cook, sew or fix things. They expected him to get a degree, work at a high-paying job and provide them with money.

"<Come on, Lai Un>," pleaded Mr. Quan, calling out to his wife by her Chinese name. "<We should go. You know how these young men are now. They want their independence. They don't want you taking care of them. Son, control your temper. I will come back this weekend and fix that door and wall for you.>"

He ushered his silent wife down the stairs. Within a few moments, they were outside. Cody could hear the engine of their Honda CRV starting. Then they pulled out of the driveway. The food and clothes that his mother was supposed to take back remained.

Cody had won the battle.

He looked around and saw the complete and utter destruction of his bathroom. It looked like a war zone. From a distance he heard his cat, Toby, meowing. The feeling of guilt started seeping in. Cody wondered if there would ever be a moment when he and his mother would get along. He was also angry at his father for letting her get away with such controlling behavior. Twenty-seven years old, he thought, twenty-seven years old and he still had to put up with this. Sometimes he wished he weren't Asian. Do other people go through this? No, he concluded, Chinese people are a unique breed of fucked up.

Cody observed the large hole in his bathroom wall and the broken bathroom door. He couldn't recognize the monster that destroyed his bathroom. After minutes of staring, he went toward his safe haven—his laptop. Computers were his drug. Ever since they had become popular during his teenage years, Cody enjoyed being in front of a monitor's warm glow. Cody opened up his email account and saw, to his surprise, a reply from Daphne.

It read:

January 23, 2005:
"Hey Cody. Thanks for the sweet email. Do you talk to all girls like this? Yes, let's meet up for sushi tomorrow at noon. I prefer Miyako's. See you then!
- Daphne."

Cody's heart skipped a beat. All traces of the angry monster had disappeared. In its place was a bright, Cheshire cat grin.

CHAPTER 3: DAPHNE LEE

Daphne Lee was both beautiful and plain looking. She was born in Beijing but grew up in the States. Her facial structure resembled a look of typical Northern Chinese origin, but her figure hinted of a consistent American diet. She had a set of large, triangular-shaped eyes, shoulder-length hair, dry lips and a round face. At five-foot-four, she was of average height. For someone who rarely worked out, her body was in terrific shape. However, as a result of her conservative attire, nothing much was revealed and what resided underneath her clothes was left for the imagination. Nothing either good or bad stood out about Daphne. Her face was symmetrical enough to resemble beauty, but any traces of charisma seemed purposely restrained. She rarely bothered with much makeup or lipstick.

"You're ten minutes late," she observed.

Cody's timing, as usual, was off. The estimated driving time from the university to Miyako Japanese Restaurant was roughly twenty minutes. Cody left his workplace ten minutes before their noon lunch appointment.

"Well, you know, there was an accident at Highway 59 and they funneled all the ongoing traffic into two lanes. That's not even counting all the construction that's been going on," Cody fumbled.

"Oh," Daphne replied.

She made no eye contact as she spoke. Her bento box was nearly empty, with just a few pieces of salad and half a tomato left. Not surprisingly, all traces of the tempura had disappeared. Daphne loved tempura, particularly the shrimp variety. She also placed things with immense precision. Her napkin was perfectly folded. Her cup of green tea was placed exactly back into the same spot. Her chopsticks, after usage, were gently returned, together in unison, near the side of her bowl. Even the wasabi, ginger and soy sauce stayed separated, unlike most sushi restaurant patrons who ignorantly mix the three together like hot pot sauce.

"Are you finished with your food already? How long have you been here?" asked Cody.

"I came twenty minutes early," she replied in her usual passive voice.

"I love this place," Cody said, giving out a slight pause. "You know they give out Miyako bucks? For every ten dollars you spend, you get one Miyako dollar. I have about a hundred of those collected. This lunch is on me."

"I already paid for it. I'm about to leave."

"Oh. That's...that's okay. Next time then. Dinner is always better for me. None of this 'rush from work' stuff."

"Um...," she replied.

Daphne looked around for the check. There was a lengthy pause.

"Yeah, so hey, I'm baptized now!" informed Cody.

"Good. That's good. I'm glad you've developed a relationship with God. That's important, you know, because we need His love to get salvation. Who shepherded you into accepting?"

"It was Ennis. He and I are childhood friends."

"Oh. Okay."

"Yeah, I was so surprised when I literally saw Jesus. It was awesome!"

"Uh-huh."

"I really haven't seen God since then though. Do you see him? Like, literally?"

Daphne hesitated to answer, "Let's just change the subject."

"Here you are," interrupted their waitress, a young Hispanic woman in her early twenties.

Daphne signed the credit card slip. She calculated the

number of reward points today's lunch would give her. Though Cody continued blabbering about various subjects, Daphne paid no attention to him. He was unattractive to her—too intense, too scrubby and too nerdy. He was also too short in stature and too lightweight for Daphne's taste. Most Asian men are ugly, she thought, and Cody was no different. It didn't matter to her that he was second-generation, born and raised in Houston. He would always be Asian. Secondary. Weak. Inferior.

"And what would you like, sir?" the waitress smiled.

"I'll, uh. Just...um," stammered Cody.

He found it difficult to decide between looking at the menu and Daphne picking up her belongings. He had waited a long time for this date. He was hesitant to accept that it would merely last several minutes.

"Just give me some miso soup, some edamame and a bento box," Cody answered.

Daphne stood up to leave.

"Hey wait, Daphne—"

"Sir, would that be Bento Box A, Bento Box B or Bento Box C?" inquired the waitress.

"I...I dunno. C. Let's do C, ok?...Hey, Daphne, wait—"

"Would that be chicken, beef or shrimp, sir?"

"Daphne.......Ugh!"

"Chicken, beef or shrimp, sir?"

Daphne walked out without looking back or saying good-bye. Cody felt a strong urge to chase after her, but he held back. The hostess in front told Daphne good-bye, to which Daphne smiled and replied back to the hostess.

"Sir?" the waitress repeated to him a third time.

"Chicken," he finally answered the waitress. His mind was miles away from his order. "I'm...I'm a chicken."

———

Mindy flashed a smile when Cody returned from lunch. She had brought her own food, which consisted of a home-cooked variety of chicken feet, bok choy and rice. The quantity she brought was enough to feed several people. Mindy ended up finishing it all. Once again, she proved to have a monstrous appetite for an extremely thin girl.

"Hey, Bubblehead!" she laughed.

"Wha—what'd you just call me?" Cody asked.

"Yeah, you got a big head, man!"

"You mean bobblehead," he corrected her.

He started browsing through his emails, hoping that Daphne would return a thank-you. There wasn't one.

"What's a bobblehead?" she inquired.

"That's like those doll things with the giant…just google it," Cody said.

"How do you spell it?"

"I don't fucking know."

An immediate feeling of guilt crept into Cody's conscience. He obviously knew how to spell "bobblehead," but he just wanted Mindy to leave him alone.

Cody decided to remedy the situation by creating conversation with her, "So what's Rachel got you doing today?"

"I just got to do some more tutorials. Hey, do you know how to make an online shopping cart?" she asked.

"Your tutorial is an e-commerce site?!" Cody asked in disbelief.

"No. I know people. They are in Taiwan. They have a shipment. There is a lot of stuff to sell. Maybe you can build a shopping cart. I will split with you. We will BE RICH!!!" she exclaimed.

"Not interested," Cody declined.

"Why not? You don't want to be rich? You would rather want to be…a…a hippie?"

"No, I just want to be content. I don't need money for that."

Cody was still facing his computer screen. Suddenly Mindy whacked him in the back of his head.

"OW! What are you doing?!!" screamed Cody." Why'd you just hit me?"

"Because you are stupid! How can you say you don't want to be rich? You think you don't need money, huh?" Mindy said.

She was a hundred-and-eighty-degree turn from the shy, introverted person she was from the previous day.

"Don't hit me like that again, OK? That hurt."

"Yeah, right! I'm so skinny and your head is so bubble!"

"Look, I've had a bad day. Bad...lunch. Just leave me alone. If you need help, let me know," Cody said.

He started working on his day's assignment. Mindy sat at her seat observing him.

"Do you have a girlfriend?" she asked.

"Oh, my God, you're in love with me," guessed Cody.

"No, STUPID! I am married, OK? I am talking about you. You went to lunch with your girlfriend, huh?"

"Jesus, please remove this woman," he prayed under his breath.

"Huh? What did you say? Something woman? Yes, I am."

"Yeah, I went to lunch with a girl. She was rude to me. I don't think she likes me. She left right away."

"Why'd she leave you? She could get a free lunch!"

"It's not like that. I don't even know why she showed up."

"Man, she sounds weird. What is her name? How do you know her?"

"Daphne. And I met her at church."

"What? You go to a church? I am Buddhist. Have you heard of Soka Gakkai?" asked Mindy as she closed her hands, placed her palms together and imitated a gesture of meditation.

"My family is Buddhist. Especially my dad," Cody revealed.

"How nice," Mindy said. "So you are in love with a girl named Daphne. How come?"

"I dunno. She's pretty. She's trustworthy and nice. Smart. Not too wild. Asian. I like Asian girls." Cody's voice trailed off as he lost track of where he was.

"It's OK, Bubble. If it was meant to be, it was meant to be. When my husband and I met, we got married after six months."

"Six months?!"

"Yes! That is the destiny. Like a red string. You know about red string?"

The red string Mindy was referring to was the Chinese version for soul mate. It was a figurative thread in which two souls were bound together. Regardless of how far apart they were, this red string would inevitably pull the two souls back together, like a rubber band.

"I believe in Jesus," Cody said with conviction. "Daphne is a God-fearing woman and I know she'll make a great girlfriend because God will lead her decisions. If two people in Christ are together, God will make it work."

Mindy reacted with a burst of laughter, covering her mouth with a ladylike politeness. However, she couldn't help but maintain eye contact.

"Ahahahahahaha!" she laughed. "Why do you think like that? She is just a woman like any other woman. Oh, Bobbie! You are such a Bobbie-Bubblehead!"

"I'm serious," countered Cody. "You should see her lead Sunday school. Her heart's in the right place."

"That's so silly, man! She is just a regular person. She is pretty, eh?"

"I think she is. But she doesn't smile enough. And she always glares at people. Like this." Cody imitated Daphne's judgmental glare.

"What? She doesn't seem like such a nice person," reasoned Mindy.

"She's a nice person. Girls from church are always nice people."

"Yeah, right. Is she born here?"

"No. She moved here early on. You know, come to think of it, I don't know much about her."

"So she is American like you. Does she speak Chinese?"

"Yeah. She's very fluent in Mandarin. She was born in China," explained Cody.

"She is from Mainland China? Be careful, Bobbie. Mainland Chinese people cannot be trusted."

Cody knew what Mindy meant by the Mainland

Chinese mentality. As a frequent visitor to Hong Kong, a city soaked with Western values from decades of British rule, he had seen firsthand the decline of moral values whenever he crossed over the Mainland Chinese border. Crime was high. Once, he was even mugged there by children no older than ten years. And, Cody had observed, the people there drove with little regard for traffic rules and safety. His Hong Kong relatives had constantly told him that Mainland Chinese people were savages. Mindy, a native of the sovereign nation Taiwan, had similar experiences with the Mainland Chinese as Cody. Much like the people of Hong Kong, the Taiwanese also held a negative image of the Mainland Chinese people.

"Stop calling me Bobbie," Cody paused. "No, she grew up here. She doesn't have Mainland Chinese traits."

"Maybe her parents they teach her the bad things," Mindy stereotyped.

"It doesn't matter. She is Christian. She knows right from wrong."

"I don't think so. I don't think she is different from any other person."

With that spoken, Cody and Mindy dropped the subject. Their conversation evolved into Mindy's daily tutorials. She was in awe of the Adobe Photoshop software's basic features like the lens flare and drop shadow effects. Particularly interesting to her was the feather effect, where the edges of an image were softened from a defined border. Cody was impressive to Mindy. He was smart, creative and energetic. Everything he did felt magical to her. By their second day together, she had already felt comfortable with Cody. Mindy was comfortable enough to lean her head on his shoulder while he explained certain aspects of the tutorial. Whoever this Daphne girl was, she thought, must be lucky to have someone like Cody chasing after her.

———————

Pastor Quentin Washington arrived with grand flair to Second Chinese Baptist Church on Wednesday afternoon. He got out of a limousine along with an entourage of other well-dressed black men in suits and sunglasses. They were mostly clergymen from his former church.

"Dang!" shouted Felix, who was painting one of the outer walls.

"Hey, how're ya doing?" greeted the smiling Pastor Washington.

The new pastor was in his late forties. He looked more like a hip-hop mogul than a man of God.

"What th—?" asked Felix.

"Pastor Washington!" greeted Pastor Lu's voice from behind, "so glad you could make it! Welcome to Second Chinese Baptist Church! Come on in. Let me give you guys a tour."

Pastor Lu was dressed in an unflattering combination of a cowboy hat, a tacky white T-shirt and jeans. The contour of his large belly was visible. Felix observed the strange contrast between the well-dressed black men and the suppressed nervousness of the Chinese congregation. However, not a bit of uncomfortable feeling was visible with Pastor Lu. He began showing his new friends around the church.

"And this stage," Pastor Lu proudly expressed, "also doubles as a baptism pool."

Several of the church members removed key floor boards from the stage, revealing a small pool for baptism. Pastor Washington and his entourage were impressed.

"Now, what about the stage lighting?" asked the new pastor. "Is there a way to dim the overall brightness and focus on the center of a stage? You know, like for dramatic effect and what not?"

"That can be arranged. Our technicians are very talented. A lot of them are electrical engineer graduates, you know," gloated Pastor Lu.

"Excellent. That's excellent," smiled Pastor Washington, scanning the large worship hall. "This is a beautiful church, Willy."

"Thank you. Thank you."

"I mean, you told me you guys don't even have a choir yet. Well, we got a whole choir we can bring...imagine a choir on that stage. Wouldn't that be something!"

A middle-aged Chinese woman, accompanied by Luke, approached the visitors with a plate of snacks.

"Would you like some cookies?" she asked the visitors.

"Oh, yes. Thank you," replied one of Washington's clergymen.

"This is my lovely wife and my son Luke. You mentioned in your letter that you have a child of your own, Quentin?" Pastor Lu asked.

"Why, yes," said Pastor Washington, gobbling on a cookie, "just my teenage daughter, Maple. They grow up so fast. My wife and I don't know what to do with her. You gotta have eyes on children at all times!"

"Oh, I know. We were lucky that Luke wasn't trouble at that age," smiled Pastor Lu.

"How old are you, my man?" asked Pastor Washington.

"Twenty-six, sir," answered Luke.

"Well, well, well. Time to get you a wife! We've got a lot of new God-obedient women that are gonna join soon. Got plenty of girls to introduce to you, son," joked the new pastor.

Polite laughter filled the room.

The rest of the tour included the Bible study halls, the library, the kitchen, the dining area, the day care centers, the indoor basketball court and, finally, the new office for Pastor Washington. The hip new pastor flashed a big, bright smile. He looked at various members of his clergy entourage and they telepathically expressed their heartfelt approval.

"It's yours," offered Pastor Lu. "Welcome to your new home, Pastor Quentin Washington."

Toby looked at Cody with an understanding only a cat owner would appreciate. The overweight gray tabby forced her way into his lap and made an intensive vibration with her purring, wagging her tail in a slow and devious pattern. Toby was very selective about when she wanted physical contact. However, she could also be a very affectionate pet when she wanted to cheer someone up. She knew by Cody's unusual silence that he was feeling distraught. As owner and pet, they had developed a psychic bond. It was this perfect balance of independence and well-timed affection that made Cody a fan of cats. What many others perceived as attitude from them, Cody saw it as an understanding of personal space.

Three nights had gone by since Daphne's lunch with Cody. He had sent a short thank-you email to her, hoping to lure a response in return. When she didn't reply back, he sat next to his house phone, contemplating calling her. Phone calls were Cody's weakness. There was something about putting a cold piece of machinery next to his ear that discouraged him from conversation. He preferred face-to-face. Cody started jotting down bullet points on some topics to bring up. He wanted to ask what she thought about God, what her favorite spots in Houston were, cooking, current events and whether or not she enjoyed fine art.

Taking a deep breath, Cody picked up the phone and dialed Daphne's cell number. There was a brief pause as the telephone lines connected. Fear started to grip Cody. What if she were on the phone with somebody else right now? he wondered. What if she's sleeping? What if another man answered the phone? What if—.

"Hello?" answered Daphne.

"Hey, Daphne. It's me, Cody. I just wanted to see if you're okay."

"Um...what do you want?"

"Nothing. I haven't heard from you since we last had lunch. We hardly talked and my emails went unanswered."

"Oh, yeah. I was busy. Sorry," she said, without a hint of remorse.

Cody decided to play the church angle.

"So, you did pretty well last time at Bible study. I really

liked your points regarding Corinthians. The definition of love is so deep and really makes us think about society's shallow definition of love. You made a good point about connecting with one another as brothers and sisters of Christ," Cody flattered.

"Yeah. Thanks."

There was a long pause.

"You know, I see Jesus sometimes. Am I crazy or do you see him too?" asked Cody.

"I used to. I used to see him all the time."

"What does that mean? He stopped showing up?"

Daphne ignored his question. "That's good that you see him, Cody. I'll pray that you see him some more."

"What about you? Anything I should pray for on your behalf?"

Daphne let out a long condescending laugh. There was another long
pause of silence.

"Let's just drop the subject, Cody."

"Okay. So, you live alone, right?" he inquired.

"Yeah," she answered.

"Any pets?"

"No."

"I live alone too. I've got a cat."

"Ew. Why do you own a cat? Most people own dogs."

"That shouldn't mean I should own a dog just because of it."

"Yeah, it should. There's a reason so many people own dogs. They're friendly, they're outgoing, they're cute and they're smart."

"I don't know," disagreed Cody. "I think they're a bit overrated. I had a Dalmatian for ten years. Well, he was more like the family dog since I didn't take care of him that much. But he was always overly eager, knocked things around, stunk, made the house dirty...just felt more annoyed about him than any other emotion. My dad loved him though. I felt sad the day the dog had to be put to sleep. It was like a family member died."

"Aw."

"Okay. Well, anyway, I'm just calling to let you know

that I think you're very attractive and that's why I want to ask you out to dinner with me."

"I know. You already told me all this on the emails, remember?"

"Sure, but you haven't responded much and I thought since we had lunch at least—"

"That's flattering, but I don't feel that way about you. I only like white guys, Cody. I'm sorry. That's just my preference."

"You and every other Asian woman," muttered Cody.

"Excuse me?"

"Nothing," Cody paused," I just want to get to know you a bit. It's, like, every time I pass by you in church, my heart starts fluttering."

"Oh."

"But I have to hide that feeling in front of others because it's weird. They'll start thinking I'm not into you for Christlike reasons. But I don't know how to approach you and tell you in any other way," Cody confessed.

"I see," Daphne replied.

"Maybe all I want to do is know you. I don't know anything about you besides the basic stuff like you sometimes lead Sunday school or that you do investing. You're a year younger than I am, and you graduated with honors from UT. But I don't know what movies you like, your favorite color or why you choose to drive that dorky Volkswagen Passat."

"That's flattering, Cody. It really is. It's sweet that you want to get to know me," she paused. "Tell you what, I'll let you be my friend. Friendship is forever. You can hear about my problems, things like my favorite color
and stuff. That could work for me."

"Oh. Okay, well, of course. We've got to be friends first, right? Yeah, we could get to know one another. Be there for each other," Cody convinced himself.

"Exactly. It'll be like that TV show *Will and Grace*," assured Daphne.

"Yeah."

There was a slight pause in conversation.

"Well. It's ten o'clock. I guess I should be getting ready for bed," she said.

"I enjoyed talking with you as well. Let's hope that this is a start of a beautiful, new friendship. And hopefully it'll blossom into something more," he hoped.

"Let's just be friends, Cody. Good night!"

CHAPTER 4: FAMILY

"Don't end up in the friend zone," lectured a stern Duke.

The seminar was held at the smallest conference room in the Doubletree Hotel near the Galleria area. It was attended by an assortment of socially awkward men, most of them Asian-American in their mid-twenties to late thirties. It was his fifth annual Alpha Asian Boot Camp—the most highly attended thus far. The objective of the seminars was to empower these men by converting them into his definition of an alpha male. Cody was also in attendance because of the deal he had made a few weeks earlier.

"Repeat what I just said," Duke barked.

"WE DO NOT END UP IN THE FRIEND ZONE," the attendees shouted in unison.

"Women are our prey. We are, by nature, hunters. Civilized society has made us forget that! This is particularly true if you're an Asian male! Look at the media! Look at what people are saying! White guys laugh at us and take our women! We fight back with stronger game! What did I just say?"

"WE FIGHT BACK WITH STRONGER GAME!"

"Good. First, I'll start by saying what I've said in all these boot camps. Forget romantic fluff. Women measure a man by three things: looks, money and social status. Be honest with yourselves. How many of you have all three? None? I bet for most of you money isn't a problem. You're Asian. You've graduated from top schools, earning good pay, and I know that's true because you're attending this class and paying thousands of dollars for it. You're making me, an alpha male, rich! But you were never taught the fundamentals of what women want. So, continuing what we've been learning, I'm introducing a method called screening," Duke said.

Duke paused so that his students could jot down the word "screening" onto their notes or laptops.

"AMANDA! Come out here," he ordered.

A beautiful blonde woman approached the stage. She had gorgeous hair that fell down to her waist, complemented by her sparkling blue eyes and magnificent smile.

"As you've all noticed, this woman is a perfect ten," explained Duke. "What are most of you? Twos, threes, a four at best. Even I'm a nine-point-five. Amanda? She's a ten. Some of you right now can't even stay conscious looking at her. So what do you do when you see a gorgeous woman like this in a bar?"

A few hands slowly went up. Duke pointed at one of them.

"Kino," suggested the student.

"Kino" was the method of touching a woman during conversation. This was to make her react and imply sexual tension.

"No," replied Duke.

"Negs," blurted another one.

"Negs" was the method of insulting a woman, breaking down her self-confidence. It was the preferred method for jerks.

"Did I point at you?" Duke scowled.

"Sorry," the second student replied.

"No. We don't use negs in this instance."

Duke glanced at the front row until he found whom he considered a weak-looking person.

"You," he said, pointing at the student, "what do you think?"

"We use screening," the student replied. "That's what you just said we're gonna learn, wasn't it?"

The students collectively laughed. Duke did not like to be made fun of. He approached the meek student and gave him a primal stare.

"Yeah. The answer is screening. Good. What's your name?" asked Duke.

"M...Minh," he answered nervously.

"Stand up," Duke commanded.

Minh did as he was told. Duke proceeded to grab him in the crotch, sending Minh screaming in pain. There was a collective wincing among the other students.

"Do you know what I'm doing to you right now?" Duke asserted.

The student fumbled for an answer, but only inaudible words came out of his mouth.

"Right now, I'm squeeeeezing your dick," informed Duke. "You like that? You like having your dick squeezed?"

Minh shook his head.

"Listen to me and listen to me well. Until the day you're alpha enough to teach this class and not give smartass remarks, I'll stop squeezing your dick. Do you understand?"

Minh nodded in pain. Duke let go of his groin and dismissed him back to his seat.

"Screening," Duke continued, "is making a woman earn you by giving her a trial of tests. Apply this when you're dealing with a ten. Watch."

The blond woman pretended to be someone in a bar. Duke paced back and forth, looking at her, determining if she were worthy of his liking.

"Hello," he said to Amanda, "I'm interested in you. Can I have your number?"

"Ugh," pretended Amanda, "why should I give it to you?"

Duke frowned.

"It's okay. Fine. That's your choice. But just know that if I give you mine, I won't answer you if you call me five times a day. It's beyond my standard."

"What?"

"Yes, even with a beautiful woman like yourself," said Duke, "I have policies. And I only like women who dress in yellow, teal green or mahogany."

"Wow!" she exclaimed, "I've never met anyone like you

before. I can meet those standards!"

"Can you? I don't think you can."

"Please, give me a chance," pleaded Amanda. "I'm begging you. You
must be an alpha male."

"I am," Duke replied.

He held her close, applying kino, then stronger kino, and finally, maximum kino. When he had her close to him, he unleashed a primal stare. Amanda felt an overflow of wetness inside her panties. A collective "wow" came from the audience.

"Psychopath," coughed Cody.

"Okay, everyone," Duke said, "take a ten-minute break. Use it wisely. Underneath your chairs is a package of Pick Up Artist guidelines and accessories. Like karate, you will seek to ascend into various levels of PUA until you become a master, or what we call an alpha PUA. Memorize the acronyms. Alpha males use acronyms to save time. There's also a chart with a formula for measuring yourself on the ladder. Looks, money and social status. Where does she fit? How does she accurately rank in a scale of one to ten? How do you rank? Can you get the ones who are ranked eight or above? Learn the secrets. Develop your day game. Then night game. Use words as an opening and then unleash various techniques to establish your dominance. Remember, women are our prey. They are to be chased, conquered and enjoyed."

During the break, Cody walked toward Duke.

"That was all bullshit!" Cody exclaimed. "I can't believe people pay you for this!"

Duke shrugged.

He turned his back towards Cody. There was no end of admirers who surrounded Duke with Pick Up Artist questions. They were fascinated by his knowledge in the art of seduction. Duke's methods involved the biological nature of animals, explained and tested through the methods of calculus and statistics. He felt it was his way of giving back to Asian men. Duke believed he gave them empowerment.

———————

"Aiya!!!!!"

It was the eve of the Lunar New Year. Cody's mother stared at his father with daggers in her eyes. Marie Un-Mui Wong had been married to Kelvin Min-Lo Quan for twenty-seven years. She had hoped that certain flaws about him would have changed since then.

"<Why did you rearrange every furniture around the house?>" she questioned. "<What's this plant doing in the middle of our kitchen? Why'd you put these cheap battery-operated glowing lotuses everywhere? Our wedding photo upstairs...it's moved!>"

"<This is proper feng shui>," Mr. Quan explained. "<I am directing as much positivity as I can.>"

"<What? No! Put it all back! You're being a ninny>," replied Cody's mother.

Their house was already compact. Bookshelves and display cases caused the narrow living spaces to be even tighter. It was located in a decent neighborhood with children constantly playing outside, where the home association did a fine job of keeping it in pristine condition.

"<What's going on?>" asked Ace Wong, scurrying downstairs.

Ace was Marie's nephew, a visa-carrying student from Hong Kong. He had been staying with them for the past two years.

"<Your uncle is being overly superstitious again>," explained Cody's mother.

"<Luck is not a superstition>," Mr. Quan defended. "<We are controlling our destiny by mastering the flow of our chi.>"

"<Do you need help?>" inquired Ace.

"<Please don't encourage him>," Cody's mother replied.

As a staunch follower of commercialized Chinese Buddhism, Kelvin Quan revolved his life around it. This meant a minimal focus on traditional Buddhist practices like meditation and mantras. Instead, he had a deep fascination for fortune-telling, charms, numbers, chi and, of course, feng shui. He felt that the fabric of their world was like a safe that could be cracked by a metaphysical master. The answer, he believed, involved proper usage of the elements, timing it with the Chinese lunar calendar, understanding its relations to the four directions, controlling it with karma and then applying any other kooky personal theory he could throw in there. This was what Cody's father loved about mainstream Buddhism; it was like a Lego set that could be assembled any way he saw fit.

"<How much did you spend on these?>" she inquired, referring to the dozens of metallic pinwheels her husband had purchased from the art store.

"<Six dollars>," he lied.

"<You liar! Why do you always buy crap like this? Is that a rocking horse?>"

"<It's a red rocking horse. It'll speed up the flow of our earth energy,
which is what we lack in this household.>"

"<Earth energy...>" Cody's mother repeated.

"<Yes. It'll ease up our surplus of fire element energy. See? The pinwheels are fanning out the bad luck. Can you get a Sharpie and help me paint them black?>"

"<This is crazy>," she criticized. "<We do this every year and our luck is still shit.>"

"<But we're close to getting it right. I can feel it. Haven't you noticed a reduction in bad incidents year after year?>"

"<I was hoping it was because you were learning your lesson from all that silly scheming. So, are we going to the temple or what? It's almost seven o'clock. It's going to be packed the closer we get toward lunar midnight.>"

Her husband agreed. Not long afterwards, both of them headed toward their local temple, which consisted of a large series of shrines devoted for mass worshipping. Because it was Lunar New Year's Eve, massive numbers of visitors came to maximize their luck. In Houston, the majority of the Asian population was an entangled mixture of Chinese and Vietnamese. The temple's crowd reflected this, with both languages intertwined among the cacophony of conversations. More noticeable was the massive amount of smoke created by the incense. Visitors grabbed handfuls of the incense to give offering to the various gods.

"<Hey!>" screamed Cody's mother.

She was about to take some incense of her own when a middle-aged woman pushed past her, grabbing handfuls of incense herself.

"<Don't be greedy!>" Cody's mother continued. "<You don't need that much luck!>"

"<Get the hell out of my way!>" the woman retorted.

"<She took all the incense and now there's none left for the rest of us! >" She glared at her husband. "<Do something!>"

"<Er...uh...excuse me, miss. Uh...>" Mr. Quan's voice trailed off.

Cody's mother chased down the woman and began pulling some of the incense away from her. She successfully wrestled a handful.

"<Gimme that!>" she yelled in conquest.

"<Let's not...please...let's not cause a scene. It's the new year>," pleaded Cody's father.

"<We needed incense!>" Cody's mother claimed.

She handed some of it to her husband. "<Here. Start clockwise from the left and I'll move counterclockwise from the right. We'll cover more gods that way.>"

The couple weaved through the large crowd efficiently, placing incense in each of the large pots per Buddhist deity. There was Shui Wei Sheng Niang, the waterfront goddess. Mazu, the protector of the sea. Zao Shen, the lord of the kitchen. Budai, the laughing Buddha. Various deified Chinese lords. The eight immortals. And finally, Guan Yin, the goddess of compassion. Of all these, she was Mr. Quan's most revered bodhisattva.

"<A wife>," he prayed to Guan Yin, "<please give my son a wife. And health. And also, I could use a winning scratch-off lottery ticket every now and then.>"

"<Are we done?>" complained Cody's mother. "<Our clothes smell like barbecue.>"

"<We still have to do some kau chim>," he insisted.

Kau chim is a fortune-telling technique that features hundreds of marked sticks in a long cup. The user prays and repeatedly shakes the cup at a forty-five degree angle until a stick falls to the ground. The user then picks up two wooden blocks and drops them to the ground. If both blocks land facing up or down, it means that the gods approve of the destiny foretold by the stick. However, if the blocks land facing differently from each other, the user has to repeat the process.

"<This is important>," muttered Mr. Quan. "<I wish our son was here for this.>"

"<Just do it for him>," Cody's mother advised.

He kneeled in front of the god statue and shook the cup. Because he was clumsy, multiple sticks fell out at once.

"<Oh, man.>" Mr. Quan hastily picked them up and tried kau chim again.

"<Hurry up and do it right, asshole!>" someone in line shouted.

Mr. Quan tried it again, this time shaking the cup more gently. This time, a lone stick fell down. He picked it up and, using his reading glasses, viewed the number written on it.

"<Number forty-one>," Cody's father read.

They went to the shelf that contained various stacks of pink paper. Each of the stacks was marked with a specific number. Mr. Quan picked up a slip from stack number forty-one.

"<What does it say?>" asked Cody's mother.

"<It's a medium luck one. 'The path you are embracing shall soon meet a fork in the road'>," he read. "<I wonder what that means? That boy better not be getting into any trouble. I think it'll be safer to buy a couple extra pinwheels tomorrow. Just in case.>"

Minutes later, the middle-aged couple walked out of the crowded, smoky temple. They were reminiscing about their early days of dating. She first met him when he was a bank clerk in the North Point district of Hong Kong. Kelvin Min-Lo Quan called her the cutie cat. She looked so young and so beautiful. Even to this day, Cody's mother continued to look ten years younger than she was. Min-Lo was quite the charmer as a teenager. He was adored by plenty of young women who claimed that he resembled Cantopop singer Sam Hui. More importantly, the young Mr. Quan was charming, nice and talkative. However, after years of marriage, his confidence deteriorated when he learned that his pretty cutie cat wife was also a feisty, domineering woman. That was fine for him, though, since his submissive personality led him to fear confrontations.

"<I wonder if he has a girlfriend already>," he wondered. "<I've never seen him with a girl. Do you think our son could be gay?>"

"<Well, he did drive to Montrose several weeks ago>," quipped Cody's mother.

Montrose is a famous gay and lesbian part of Houston.

"<Wasn't that for work though?>"

"<Why would he need to drive anywhere for his work?>" she reasoned. "<He sits in front of a computer all day for his job.>"

"<Our son's not gay>," Mr. Quan confidently believed. "<He can't be. Besides, I'd rather he'd be a homosexual than someone who married a black person. I would disown him if he did that.>"

"<He wouldn't marry a black girl>," assured Cody's mother.

"<I know. But if he did. I'd disown him. I would.>"

"<How about a white girl?>"

"<Oh! Now that...that'd make me happy!>" he glowed. "<Our grandchild would be so beautiful. We'd be so rich.>"

"<I'd honestly rather he'd married a white girl over an Asian one>," she admitted.

"<It doesn't matter to me. You know how I am. I love everyone. But no blacks.>"

Cody's father heard his cell phone ringing. The number was from the hospital. Why would they suddenly be calling me at eight o'clock? he wondered.

"Hello?...........yes, this is Kelvin....... yes....... okay.......please repeat, my English suck......okay.......okay.....what happened?.........I thought you said everything is okay? Now it is not okay?.........okay, okay, I'm coming."

"<What's wrong?>" asked Cody's mother.

"<Call Cody. Tell him to meet us at the hospital. My mother's health unexpectedly took a fatal turn.>"

It was midnight at the hospital when the Quan family and other family members gathered around Skinny Grandma. She was in a comatose state, "alive" by only the technical definition of the word. The unified humming and beeping from the medical equipment was heard through the family's silence. In attendance was Cody, both of his parents, a various assortment of aunts and uncles, Duke, their cousin Minston, Minston's much-too-young-for-him girlfriend Wanda, Minston's thirty-year-old ex-girlfriend, Cody's two maternal cousins Ace and Megan, and, finally, his grandfather.

The last one on that list was the most notable in attendance.

It was rare for Cody's paternal grandparents to be in the same place together. For reasons never entirely explained to them, he and his paternal cousins were unclear about why his grandmother held a lifelong grudge against his grandfather. He knew that they had never married, but even in the most contemporary of Chinese culture, couples joined together anyway for the sake of unison. This was especially true for his grandfather's generation. Therefore, an appearance by the elderly man was an indication that Skinny Grandma was lying on her deathbed.

"<Passing away at Chinese New Year, mother>," cried Mr. Quan. "<How perfect is fate?>"

"<Don't be ridiculous, Min-Lo! >" shouted his older sister Mei. "<How do you know this is it?>"

Cody's Aunt Mei was always bossing around his father. Both Cody and his mother resented her. She was bullheaded, loudmouthed and domineering. There was no doubt she had passed on those values to her son Duke.

"<Because the doctor said so!>" Cody's mother retorted.

"<Yeah? Well, I don't trust that Mexican man>," exclaimed Aunt Mei.

"<Oh, why couldn't they have given mother a white doctor? They must want her to die!>"

Mr. Quan nodded in agreement. "<And notice how most of the nurses are black too. This is most definitely a conspiracy.>"

Cody stood there dumbfounded. Just a week ago, the hospital staff had assured him that his grandmother was going to be okay. They had claimed that the heart surgery would only be a minor risk. He had done his best to understand all the medical jargon, but that was the summary of what the doctor had explained. Cody looked at Duke to ensure that he, too, had concluded something similar from the previous doctor's meeting. Though Duke hesitated to make eye contact, the signs of confusion on his face indicated that he had thought the same.

Both of them held a deep love for their grandmother. Without her, their childhood memories would be empty. The original house that Cody grew up in was a very modest one, taken care of by Skinny Grandma. Because Aunt Mei was going through marital issues, Duke, as a child, would spend time living in the home. The old backyard had been practically turned into a farm. Row after row, the soil was used to grow melons and other assorted vegetables. Chickens and pigeons ran around. The two boys were usually sent to the nearby stables, asking local farmers for horse manure that would be used for fertilizer. The Alief area that they grew up in was a different place in the early eighties; it was slightly suburban but still had traces of ruralness. This, however, did not stop either Cody or Duke from proudly revealing that they were from there. Alief was their home, their childhood, their best memories. It reminded them of a time when both were as close as brothers instead of distant cousins.

"We gotta go," whined Minston's ex-girlfriend.

"No, this my grandmother!" responded Minston in broken English. "Late one hour clubbing. Okay today."

"Like we make a difference here!" she pouted. "It's my friend's birthdayyyyy!"

"Ooooh, is it held at the Roxy?" asked Minston's current girlfriend, Wanda.

"Who asked you, bitch?"

"Slut!"

Duke angrily glared at the two scantily dressed women. The one in her late thirties had a horrible boob job. The other one, Wanda, was an underaged girl who had too much makeup on but too little clothing. When she caught Duke's intimidating expression, she leaned closer toward Minston for safety.

"I think your group should leave," Duke firmly commanded.

"Come on, baby. Your cousin is scary," glared Wanda.

"Sigh," muttered an annoyed Minston. "<Okay, okay. She better not be dead when I come back tomorrow!>"

The middle-aged playboy left the room with his two lady friends.

Several hours passed. Each family member procrastinated about leaving, wondering if this would be their last chance with Skinny Grandma. Once one o'clock in the morning came, however, Cody's parents left because of Ace and Megan. His aunts and uncles slowly followed suit. Duke, Cody and their grandfather were the ones left remaining. Finally, their grandfather walked towards her and offered his condolences.

"<I'm sorry>," whispered Cody's grandfather. "<I'm so sorry for what I did to you.>"

Though both cousins were curious about what had happened between their grandparents, they were raised not to ask questions.

"<Min-Guang>," Cody's grandfather commanded to him in his Chinese name, "<Take me home>."

Duke was offended. He was the responsible one. His grandfather would be safer with him instead of his immature cousin. But then again, he wasn't a Quan. This hierarchy by birthright silently angered Duke. Out of obligation, Duke kept silent, exiting the room with them. They left Skinny Grandma, clinging on to life in her hospital bed.

As the elevator took them down, Cody observed how elegant the hospital was. His grandfather silently stood next to him, occasionally muttering a deep, regretful sigh. Whatever was going on in his head, Cody thought, was decades of history about a complicated love affair. It was one that only his grandparents knew about. Sure his parents, aunts and uncles had an idea, but it was probably a summarized version. People kept secrets, Cody surmised. People kept them to their graves.

Once they were in the parking garage, both cousins walked their separate ways.

"You remembered where you parked?" asked Cody.

Duke ignored him and continued walking.

"Okay then," continued Cody, "drive safely. Remember……family dinner tomorrow for Chinese New Year."

Duke felt insulted that his cousin would remind him of things like Chinese New Year. In his mind, he believed that he was more Chinese than Cody would ever be. Duke had values. He had tradition and cultural pride. Cody once joked that they weren't really Chinese because neither of them could name three streets in China. Duke countered that blood decided their nationality. The terms Chinese-American or Asian-American were acceptable, but never just American. The latter symbolized integration, an idea Duke couldn't accept.

Once Duke found his car, he sat in it for a few seconds. He had never been a spiritual or religious person, but for a mere moment he realized it was no good being an atheist either. He cried and mumbled words that resembled prayers. They were wishes to whatever cosmic forces were out there listening. When it came to Skinny Grandma, Duke would do anything, believe in anything, to save her.

———————

It didn't take long for Cody to drop his grandfather off at his retirement complex. Before his grandfather left the car, however, he had a few words for Cody.

"<Please take time to have dinner with me more often>," he insisted. "<Out of all my grandchildren, I love you the most. You are the last remaining Quan. Whatever is mine is yours. Please know that, Min-Guang.>"

"<Yes>," Cody replied.

His grandfather continued, "<You're a good boy. I hope you are obedient. You should find a wife and make some grandchildren to honor me. I would be most happy if you married your cousin in Hong Kong.>"

There was an awkward pause.

"<But improper cousin not love>," protested Cody in broken Cantonese.

"<Improper? What's so improper about it?>" wondered his grandfather. "<Back in my village, everyone married their cousins. Is she not pretty enough for you? Why must you be so picky? It's not like she's your sister.>"

"<Girlfriend already have I.>"

"<Oh, really, you have a girlfriend? Who? Is she Chinese? She must be Chinese, Min-Guang.>"

"<Yes. Beijing born she original.>"

"<Ah! A Beijing girl! That's good! Very good. She can cook dumplings for you!>"

"<No but raise must her in America small since.>"

"<Huh? I didn't understand what you just said.>"

"<She no cook.>"

"<What do you mean she doesn't cook? That's a woman's job.>"

"<Invest. She does.>"

"<I see. Well, maybe when you're both married she can stay home and cook for you.>"

There was a moment of silence.

"<I am tired, Min-Guang>," Cody's grandfather continued. "<I love your grandmother, but things didn't go well between us. I did much to make up for the mistakes of my youth. So, I'm still disappointed and confused why she never forgave me. We could have been a more unified family.>"

"<What happened?>"

Cody's grandfather paused for an answer.

"<Sometimes, small things can seem like bigger things, Min-Guang>," explained his grandfather. "<In the end, they don't matter. Behave and always be obedient. Consider marrying your cousin. That is the best advice I can give you. Good night, Min-Guang.>"

Cody observed his grandfather as he walked into the retirement home's entrance. He had always watched because he never knew if it would be the last time he'd see him. His grandfather was nearly eighty-five years old. Cody was very blessed to see him in such peak health. This brought his mind back to his grandmother in the hospital. The doctors had estimated that she might not make it past the current month. More so, it seemed to Cody that she might not even make through the night. What if, he wondered, she would pass away in a few hours? What if this was his last chance?

Fearing this, Cody drove back to the hospital. Once he was there, he observed his grandmother in her hospital room. There she was, full of tubes and IVs, clinging on to the very end of her life. She looked frail and mortal. He reached out to hold her hand. There was no reaction. He crudely estimated that Skinny Grandma had probably only a five-percent chance of living at this point. Cody realized what he had to do. He kneeled beside his grandmother and sought a higher power.

"Jesus," he prayed, "dear Jesus, save her. Please. I love her."

Cody said it with tears streaming down his closed eyes. He cried until it became audible.

"Okay," he heard a voice say.

Cody opened his eyes and saw Jesus standing across the other side of the bed. He was wearing green hospital scrubs. The medical equipment began beeping louder in unison. Jesus winked at Cody.

"<Min-Guang?>" asked Skinny Grandma suddenly.

She had awakened in full health.

"Thank you," smiled a cheerful Cody. "Thank you!"

"<Min-Guang, who are you talking to?>" asked his grandma.

"<Jesus did I talk to>" he stammered in broken Cantonese.

"<Jesus? That's silly, Min-Guang. We're Buddhist.>"

CHAPTER 5: IN LOVE, IN FAIRNESS

A new scene was awaiting the usual congregation of Second Chinese Baptist Church. For the first time, its large parking lot exceeded full capacity. People were slowly being funneled into its welcoming doors like streams of water flowing into a drain. Most apparent was the unusual mix of Asian and black attendants scattered about, keeping a combination of distance and politeness. Both groups were in stark contrast with one another. The Asian crowd were clad in a near-uniform attire—mostly black suits, white shirts and an assortment of ties for the men; long-sleeved white dresses for the women. The African-American crowd, on the other hand, wore an assorted array of colorful outfits, like a bag of Skittles scattered around the church. Most notable were the fancy hats of the elderly black women. The Asian and black children were sent to the nursery where their color blindness allowed them to mingle without hesitation. The adults, on the other hand, were distracted by their differences, enough to divert their attention from the day's message delivered by the new pastor, Quentin Washington.

"From one man," boomed the affluent black preacher, "He made all the nations, that they should inhabit the whole earth. And he marked out their appointed times in history and the boundaries of their lands. Acts 17:26."

The church was packed to its maximum capacity.

For several weeks, Pastor Lu had been announcing the addition of a new pastor to the current Chinese membership. What he had understated to them, however, were how many new people would immediately join, and more shockingly, that all of them were black.

"<From one man>," followed the translator in Mandarin Chinese, "<He made all the nations, that they should inhabit the whole earth. And he marked out their appointed times in history and the boundaries of their lands. Acts 17:26.>"

To the Chinese crowd, having sermons interrupted for a translation was commonplace in an Asian church. However, the black crowd was far from used to it, and it silently irritated many of them that they were getting pauses in between the pastor's delivery. Some in the black audience also wondered if there had always been a security guard sitting near the front door.

"Since the days of Babel," continued Pastor Washington, "God has made us different. We look different, we speak different languages, we have different tastes. Similarities make us cocky. Makes us self-righteous. But DIVERSITY. Diversity humbles. God may have made us into the image of Him, but we are scattered pieces of Him, like a puzzle. Only by working together and being together can we see a fuller image of Jesus."

"Amen!" "Amen!" "Hallelujah!" shouted various members from the black crowd.

Several of the Chinese congregation looked around and then at one another. Daphne glared at one particular black woman who started shaking up and down like she was being possessed.

"Just look around," insisted the pastor. "Look around and let yourselves know that this...this was meant to be. God doesn't want a bag of flavorless tortilla chips. No. He wants an assorted party mix of Doritos."

"Doritos?" Marco Ling angrily mumbled to himself.

"AMENAMENAMEN!!!" came a squeaky high-pitched male voice.

It was from Herman Shu, a skinny, overly active young member of the Chinese youth congregation. Herman came to church services in spurts. A self-proclaimed prodigy, he liked to view himself as an intellectual, making a habit out of debating and interrupting as many conversations, lectures or events as possible. He was known to love attention. No one quite remembered when Herman had joined the congregation, though he had been there for a very long time. His personal history was a blurry one, and the numerous explanations of his origins contradicted themselves.

"Uh, thank you," replied Pastor Washington. "As I said...today, as we see ourselves as brothers and sisters in Christ, the Almighty, the Lord, the Man Upstairs, just by being together, Chinese and black, we are already doing His work."

"PREACH ON, BROTHER! OHHHHH WEEEEEE!" Herman stood up and started doing a spin dance.

"Herman! Please sit down!" hissed Ennis.

"You sure are pumped up today," chuckled the elderly black woman next to Herman.

The sermon extended past the hour because of the translations. It ended with Luke leading a small band, which was comprised of acoustic guitars and the soft, soprano voice of Henry. After awhile, it transitioned to a makeshift choir group from Washington's previous church. Many of the new black members clapped and shouted at the top of their lungs. Cody stood and watched several of the Chinese members join them, even when their mimicking revealed a lack of familiarity toward such an openly emotional style of worship.

Finally, Pastor Lu concluded the service in prayer.

"Dear Heavenly Father. We do not know why you have put us together...this, unique...combination of Christians. But we have faith that this is your plan. We thank you for Pastor Washington. Thank you for the challenge of having a larger church. May we grow together and learn about you through these times. May we set an example of what this can accomplish when we put our differences aside and bask in your love. In Jesus' name we pray, amen."

The congregation followed with a collective amen.

"Are you sure you're married?" asked Cody.

"Yes. I am," replied Mindy.

"Then explain to me why the two of us are sharing a table at a five-star steakhouse on Valentine's Day?"

It was the night afterwards: Valentine's Day. Del Frisco's was one of the most expensive steakhouses in Houston, next to Taste of Texas and Perry's, both of which Cody had always believed to be overrated. Located at the side of the famous Galleria mall, it was constantly filled, but never more so than this special holiday for lovers.

"Because you wanted dinner, Bubblehead," Mindy said, browsing through the menu. The menu was short, following the restaurant rule that the higher the class of the restaurant, the fewer choices available.

"Stop calling me Bubblehead. And when I said dinner, I meant Jack in the Box. Maybe Chick-fil-A," said Cody.

"That is unhealthy! Besides, you said you like turtle soup. And this is one of the few places that will have it. I want to try it!"

"So where's your husband? Why isn't HE taking you out tonight?"

"Because he's working, man!"

Cody gave her a skeptical eye.

"Why aren't you wearing a wedding ring?"

"Huh? Are you crazy? What the silly question is that? It can get stolen. I never wear it outside! Man, it's so dark in here. I cannot read the menu. They need to open the lights!"

"Okay, you're paying half. You're not my girlfriend," said Cody.

"Tsk. You make more than me! I am a student. That is not gentlemanly of you, Bubblehead!" explained Mindy.

She leaned closer to him.

Cody was lost in thought. He replayed the events earlier this Valentine's Day when he made a custom CD of carefully selected songs for Daphne. He had gone to her workplace with the CD and fruit flowers. Her initial surprise of seeing him there was quickly replaced with annoyance. She felt embarrassed. Daphne quickly shooed him out of her workplace, giving the fruit flowers to her boss instead. She then tossed the CD into the trash.

"HEY!" Mindy interrupted Cody's thought process, "I want the sixteen-ounce ribeye! That looks good!"

"Can you eat all that?! Where does it all go? You must poop a lot!"

"Ahahahahaha!" giggled Mindy.

The two new friends eventually placed their orders and enjoyed the night away. After her second glass of wine, the lightweight Mindy started feeling buzzed. She carefully glanced at Cody's face amidst the dim, flickering candlelight.

"You know what?" Mindy muttered. "You are my best friend,"

"Oh...that steak was so good. Damn. That steak was fucking good," observed Cody.

"Why do you say so many bad words? I thought you go to church."

"It's okay. I can curse."

"No, it's not, Bobbie. You must set a good example," assured Mindy.

"Oh yeah? You should come to our church some time."

"Haha. No. Church people are mean. Besides, it's so stupid. It doesn't make sense. They just want your money. Have you ever given them money?"

"No. Not yet," replied Cody.

"Good! Because that is how they trick you!"

Cody paused.

"What's your husband's name?" Cody asked her.

"I don't know. Hahaha!"

"What do you mean you don't know? You made him up, didn't you?"

"Hahaha! I'm just kidding, Bubble! His name is Wing Wei. We met singing karaoke. Hey! Wanna hear me sing? I'm good."

"You're drunk, Mindy," Cody flatly replied.

"Am I? The wine taste like grape juice, man. Sorry. HEY! Guess what?"

"What?"

"Tonight we celebrate!" Mindy held her glass toward Cody's glass.

Cody cheered her glass.

"What are we celebrating, buddy?" asked Cody.

"To our new partnership! I am making you the cofounder chief executive vice president of Mosaic Decor!" smiled Mindy.

"I told you I don't want in on any of your kooky business ideas."

"Come on! We are going to be rich! I have it all in my head! You just make the website. We sell it! Okay?"

"And how are we going to find suppliers? What is being sold anyway?"

"Home decor! But modern! That is why I have decided to call it Mosaic Decor!"

"Mosaic doesn't mean modern, dear," corrected Cody.

"It sounds cool, man. It's easy! Come on! I know some wholesalers."

"Okay, okay. Fine. I can use some side income."

Mindy grabbed Cody's hand and placed her head on his shoulder. The waiter came over and handed them their check.

"How was it? Good?" asked the waiter. "You two seem happy. How long have y'all been together?"

"We're not a couple," corrected Cody.

"Oh," paused the waiter, "should I split the check then?"

"No, no. It's alright. I got it," Cody plopped down his credit card.

"I'm already married!" exclaimed Mindy.

The baffled waiter thanked Cody and took his card back to be processed. Mindy stared at the patrons at the table next to them. An older gentlemen in his fifties was feeding chocolate cake to a giggling young woman in her twenties.

"Man," observed Mindy, "that guy. He is too old for her! And that lady, her boobs are fake!"

"Stop staring at people. It's not polite."

"You think I need some fake boobs? Mine are small. My husband give me a nickname. He calls me Ms. A-Minus!" informed Mindy, regarding her breast size.

The waiter returned with Cody's receipt.

"Thank you for dining with us at Del Frisco's. I hope you both have a VERY pleasant evening," smiled the waiter.

Mindy held on to Cody's arm as they walked out of the Galleria steakhouse. The mall was closing, but since it was Valentine's Day, it wasn't as empty as it would have been on an average Monday night. Mindy waited outside while Cody walked around the parking lot trying to find his car. The car was a six-year-old sea green 2000 Acura Integra. It was only a four-cylinder automatic, but its outward appearance made the small sports car appear faster than it was.

Cody finally found his car and drove up to where Mindy was waiting.

"Man, what took you so long?!" quipped Mindy.

They headed west along Westheimer Road—traffic was beginning to thin out for the night. Mindy played around with the radio until she found an adult contemporary station.

"Ooh! My favorite song! It's by Daniel Powter!" Mindy started singing along. "'You had a bad day! La la la la. Ma ma la la...la la la la!'"

"How can this be your favorite song? You don't even know the words."

"I like it, okay?!"

They stopped at a traffic light. A bum walked up to Cody's car, offering to clean his windows. Cody aggressively shook his head in rejection. The bum continued to clean the front window anyway.

"Hey, hey! Stop! I said no!" Cody shouted.

Cody squirted water from his windshield wipers at the bum while he was still cleaning the car window. Soaking wet, he flicked his middle finger at Cody and then extended his other hand for money.

"Give me my dolla, muthafucka!" demanded the bum.

The traffic light turned green.

"Go go go!" insisted Mindy.

Cody drove off.

"Man, why don't they get a real job? That nigger!" blurted Mindy.

"Hey! Don't say that word! It's wrong!" Cody said.

"Why not? I hear them call each other that all the time."

"You just can't. It's...it's a rule."

"Rule, huh? You always call me a fob. How come you can say fob and I can't say nigger?"

"I shouldn't be calling you a fob either."

"But you do! I don't like it when you call me that, Bobbie."

"Okay, okay. I'll stop calling you a fob."

"And I'll stop calling you a nigger."

"You didn't call me that word," insisted Cody.

"What word?" Mindy asked.

"The word that just said."

"How come you can't say it? Say it out loud!"

"No," said Cody.

"Man, this country is so sensitive, man! In Taiwan, we can laugh at those things!"

"Well, in Taiwan, everyone is...Taiwanese!" Cody reasoned.

"What do you mean by that?"

"You're all Chinese!"

"We are not all Chinese!"

"I don't mean politically," Cody said, "I mean—"

"I am not Chinese, Bubble! I am half Japanese and half Korean!"

Cody was stunned.

"Then how come you speak Taiwanese?" he asked.

"Because I grew up in Taiwan! But people can make fun of me and say Korean or Japan joking! No one is in offense!"

A long pause resulted.

Deep down inside, Cody understood what Mindy was talking about. He recalled, once again, the day he punched out the fifth-grade bully, Derrick James. Derrick James was a large black kid, two years older than the average fifth-grader. He remembered Derrick and other black kids beating him up in front of the teachers. They constantly called him several racist names, but the teachers turned the other way. When Cody finally found the courage and anger to stand up to Derrick, Cody screamed the word "nigger" for his first and only time. The school suspended him for what they dubbed "a racial incident." Cody had to apologize to Derrick's family and admit to them that he had a problem and needed help. Memories like these had long been buried. As a young adult, Cody had found closure, but Mindy's reasoning brought the topic back up.

"HEY, LOOK OUT!" screamed Mindy.

A Mexican man, trying to cross the street, suddenly ran in front of Cody's car. Cody instinctively tried to swerve past him, but it was too late. The man was airborne for a split second, landed across the windshield, and then ricocheted onto the pavement, leaving a splattering of blood on the passenger side of the windshield.

"AHHHHHHH!" screamed Mindy.

From his rearview mirror, Cody saw the motionless body lying on the street. Cody stepped on the brakes and got out of the car.

"What are you doing? Don't get out!" pleaded Mindy.

They were in a dangerous neighborhood.

Cody heard a woman scream. A round, middle-aged Hispanic lady ran to comfort the hit pedestrian. Moments later, local residents started to gather around the unconscious man. Cody stood next to him. The man was alive but in critical condition. Several of the neighbors got on their knees, praying for help. Cody slowly spun around; several Jesuses appeared at once to comfort each praying person.

"Who the fuck did this? Who da motherfucka did this?" demanded a skinny, short-haired, spunky and tomboyish teenage girl. She pointed at Cody, "You did this? You hit Gustavo?"

"Yeah, I did," answered Cody. "I just want to make sure he's fine until the ambulance comes."

"Fine? He look fine to you, dipshit?" She whipped out a knife.

"Hey, it was an accident! He shouldn't have run in front of my car!"
Cody pleaded.

"Te voy a arrancar la cabeza!" the aggressive teenage girl screamed in Spanish.

"Bobbie! HELP!" screamed Mindy from the car.

Cody looked back with terror in the direction of his car where Mindy was still inside. He saw several gangbangers surrounding it. A girl from the crowd yanked Cody aside.

"I just called 911," she explained. "Don't talk back to any of them no matter what they say. Just let them yell at you."

For ten intense minutes, Cody endured a barrage of verbal insults, most of them in Spanish. Inside the car, Mindy repeatedly dialed her husband's cell phone, but he did not answer. The bastard's sleeping, she thought. Finally, flashing red and blue lights from two police cars came to their rescue. Sirens from a nearby ambulance could also be heard.

"What's going on here?" asked one of the officers in a deep Texan twang.

"I was just driving when all of a sudden this guy tried to cross the street. He did it right in front of my car. You have to believe me, it's the truth," explained Cody.

"Oh, I believe you alright," laughed the officer. "This happens once a week in this part of Westheimer. It's always a beaner that gets hit."

"You shouldn't say that word," corrected Cody.

"Son," the officer responded, "I'm going to protect you and clear your name in this here mess. You let me say what I want. Got it?"

Paramedics soon arrived. They carted the injured pedestrian to the ambulance. Mindy and Cody were both escorted away by several policemen from the hostile neighborhood crowd.

"Y'all need a ride back home?" offered a policeman.

"Yes. Can you guys take my friend back home too?"

"She's not your wife?" asked the surprised policeman.

"No, if you had taken down my ID, you would have seen that I'm single."

"Don't worry about that," chuckled the police officer. "We know it's not your fault. Come on, where does she live and where do you live?"

"She lives in Sugar Land. I'm a few blocks away," replied Cody. "You sure you don't want to check our IDs?"

The officer sighed and took Cody and Mindy's license; both cleared.

"Bobbie, you be careful, huh? I'll see you at work tomorrow," Mindy paused. "Thanks for everything. I had a lot of fun tonight. Hope you did too. Sorry about your car."

She looked at the policeman.

"Can I sit in the front?" she insisted.

———————

Daphne felt no remorse about her treatment of Cody earlier in the day; she had already forgotten about it. Her mind was preoccupied with Valentine's Day dinner with Kyle Sawyer and his family—she had just been invited by Kyle to meet them. She had known him since her high school years when Kyle led the Clements High Rangers to successful seasons as the starting quarterback. Tall and well-built with a masculine jaw, the dreamy blue-eyed, blond-haired titan had fallen on tough times after suffering a career-ending injury near the end of his senior year in a playoff game.

Fortunately for him, Kyle was as much brains as he was brawn. He had graduated from the University of Texas with honors, double majoring in business and accounting. His academic success helped ease the pain of his athletic letdown, though a large part of him would always miss playing football. In Texas, football is king, and Kyle was once a part of that royalty. The thought of being just another face in the crowd disturbed him.

Although they had never officially dated, Daphne had

interpreted their consistently matching college class schedules as a sign from God. This made her believe that choosing to be a Texas Longhorn instead of an A&M Aggie was the right decision. She had wanted to be wherever Kyle wanted to be. And while he had several other relationships during their time as friends, Kyle was quick to pick up Daphne's passive-aggressive interest in him as a lover. He had asked her to hang out with him on several occasions, appreciating Daphne as a buddy, yet, at certain times, using her as something more. She loved him enough to give up her virginity, though she hid this fact from her family and friends. Besides, she reasoned, this man is destined to be my future husband. She didn't feel like she had sinned as a devout Christian; it was a loophole she'd found.

Hence, when Kyle asked her to join his family for dinner on Valentine's Day, Daphne was delighted. For the first time in a long time, she gave a heartfelt prayer to God. She knew it was putting the cart ahead of the horse, but during her drive to Kyle's house she pictured what their children would look like. Mixed children are so beautiful, she sighed to herself. How many boys? How many girls? Daphne wanted two of each—a family of six, living in a nice three-story home with a white picket fence.

The American dream.

"So, Daphne," smiled Kyle's mother, "thanks for tutoring Kyle with his trigonometry homework. Your math skills really came in handy."

She wore a necklace with large white pearls, which complemented her pink suit and white hair.

"Actually, Mrs. Sawyer, I helped him with his English," corrected Daphne.

"Ah!" exclaimed Kyle's mother, nudging her husband, "see, dear, these Asian kids are taking over our language now! Y'all are so smart at everything!"

Silence followed. The four of them ate their chicken, mashed potatoes and green beans. The rhythmic clinging of silverware could be heard amidst the silence.

"You know, Kyle's changing his job. He just got a job offer from NASA!" said Mrs. Sawyer.

"Oh wow! Really?" replied Daphne. "Gosh, Kyle, I'm so happy to hear that! Does that mean you're moving to the Clear Lake area?"

"Mmm," Kyle said waiting to finish chewing his food. "Well, mom exaggerates. I'm not sure I'm actually going to take it."

"What? Why not, Kyle?!" asked his mother."Surely you can't be happy doing what you're doing right now. You don't make nearly enough that matches your worth."

"I'm planning on trying out for the Canadian Football League next season," declared Kyle.

"You're doing what?" Kyle's father was surprised. "That's a bad idea."

"Kyle, you'll get hurt. You had a serious injury and you're lucky you can still walk like a normal person," reasoned a concerned Daphne.

"Yes, listen to your Asian girlfriend," said Kyle's mother.

He grew irritated. "You guys just don't understand. A large part of my soul has been missing ever since high school. I need football. I had several physical trainers evaluate and tell me I can bounce back and have a good career."

"Kyle...I—" his mother started before getting interrupted.

"It's the Canadian Football League, not the NFL. Who's ever made it to the NFL from that dismal league?" asked his father.

"Warren Moon did. Doug Flutie," answered Kyle.

"Aberrations. Statistically speaking it's one in a million. But you're your own man. You do what you want," said Mr. Sawyer. He looked at Daphne. "Or date whatever kinds of people you want."

Another long moment of silence followed.

"Soooo, Daphne. How do you like the dinner so far?"

"It's very good, Mrs. Sawyer," smiled Daphne.

"You're so polite. So where are you from? Are you Japanese or Korean?"

"I was born in Beijing. But I grew up here," Daphne replied.

"So you're Japanese. My coworker is Japanese. Her name is Oki

Mishima. She has two sons. Do you know them?"

"No, Mrs. Sawyer."

"Beijing's the capital of China," corrected her husband. "She's Chinese."

"Isn't that where your brother deployed to in the seventies?" inquired Mrs. Sawyer.

"No, that was Korea," explained Mr. Sawyer. He was getting full.

"Oh, that's right! He has an Asian wife. They met during his time there. That woman has the most beautiful skin. How do y'all keep that skin so smooth and youthful? Look at my arms, they're full of spots. Do you have some kind of secret Asian cream that you can recommend to me?" asked Kyle's mother.

Kyle got up and headed out.

"Where are you going?" asked Mr. Sawyer.

"Leaving," explained Kyle. "Gonna go to Joe's. Think we're gonna shoot the shit and drink a few."

"Well, what about your little Saigon girlfriend here?" asked his father.

"She can help mom clean the dishes. Hell if I care," Kyle shrugged heading out.

Daphne watched as he drove his car out of the driveway. He didn't even bother looking back, she noticed. Her heart sank. She felt lower than dirt.

"You know, I only buy Toyotas. They're great cars!" exclaimed Mrs. Sawyer.

Daphne glared at her.

CHAPTER 6: THE HUSTLE

The Platinum Star was celebrating its second-year anniversary as a dance club in Houston—a long lifespan for a city whose other clubs averaged six months maximum. Because of their frequent changes in ownership, most clubs were, instead, known for their locations. Though The Platinum Star wasn't a decades-long success like the Roxy, people still knew it by its name. They didn't come for its shabby decorations or its mediocre music; it was, however, a place where the best drug deals could be found.

Among its many clubbers that night was Pete Mok. Pete had been out of jail for two months, thanks to an early Christmas Day parole. It was, in his mind, an easy stay. During his stint in prison, he had the luck of being protected by Big Thunder, a large, thick-mustached Hispanic enforcer whom Pete had known from his earlier criminal career. No one had laid a hand on Pete, giving his prison experience the equivalent of an extended bed and breakfast. He had made the survival decision of shaving his head, hiding his natural curly hair. That, along with a body decorated in tattoos, had transformed Pete from looking like the guy who could get mugged to the guy doing the mugging.

Yet, word on the street suggested that Pete was still soft. He was a sheep among wolves, mostly getting by because he was well-liked. He didn't have a malicious bone in his body;

Pete's good heart, however, made up for his timidity. Also, fortunately, he had the added trait of astounding luck, making him the underworld Forrest Gump. Even his criminal peers recognized it. Since there was little for them to take from Pete, they never bothered to hustle him. They recognized him as one of their own, figuring his vulnerabilities gave him some usefulness. That was how Pete originally got into the drug dealing life. He was asked by a local supplier to store cocaine in his family home. At the time, Pete turned out to be a perfect cover for the supplier. While he lived with his mother, he hid tens of thousands of dollars' worth of drugs underneath his childhood bed and, because his household was Asian, was not suspected by police.

Eventually, though, Pete's naivety and carelessness got the better of him. He became addicted to his own supply. Moreover, he openly talked about his drug dealing career, eventually leading to his own capture. One morning, a large narcotics police force stormed into his house and forced his grandparents, little sister, cousins and mother onto the floor. They tore through his family's furniture before finding the cocaine underneath his bed. That was how Pete got caught and sent to prison. Drug dealing and burger flipping were the only two occupations he had ever known. And Pete loved the former.

The familiarity of the club scene distracted him while his good friend Danny, a Cambodian-American friend of similar age, approached the lead bartender named Li'l Bis. Li'l Bis was easily identifiable from his eye patch—a little souvenir from his Vietnam War days.

"My man Li'l Bis. How ya doin'? Brought my boy Pete for Piranha," informed Danny.

"Yeah, I know who he is, Danny. This the dumb motherfucker who got caught with drugs in his own bed," scoffed the bartender.

The grizzled, one-eyed veteran was an old friend of The Platinum Star owner, Piranha, who saved him from an encounter with the Viet Cong over forty-five years ago.

"Nigga, dun gimme that. Pete was just startin' out. Anyway, I asked Piranha to give him another chance," insisted

Pete's friend.

"What you want this life fo'? Y'all school boys. Y'all just fuck up again," replied Li'l Bis.

"We already got word he say yea, so just let us in!" demanded Danny.

"Oh, what? Y'all got an appointment? This the doctor's office now?" Li'l Bis barked back. He finished cleaning off the beer mug he was wiping. "Shiiiit. Follow me. Hope he can talk some sense into you."

The bartender led them through a narrow and dark hallway within the back of The Platinum Star. They passed by small rooms where patrons were snorting cocaine on mirrored tables. Pete recognized some of them as celebrities. Li'l Bis brought them to a large, brightly lit office whose entranceway was covered by bead curtains. In the middle of the room lay a large oak desk, occupied by two men on each end. Piranha was a physically imposing middle-aged black man, large and powerful in stature. His body language suggested deep inner strength, forged by the fires of hardened life experience. The choice of his attire included dark sunglasses, a nice white suit and a dark purple tie. Across from him was an equally well-dressed, hefty-looking Asian man, whose choice colors were black suit and beige tie. Li'l Bis removed himself from the office, closing the door behind him. The office walls absorbed most of the club sounds, giving them a resemblance of privacy for conversation.

"Yo, Piranha, man," said Danny, "thanks for giving my nigga Pete a second chance."

The drug baron collected his thoughts. There were no chairs left in the office for either of them, so they remained standing.

"My family," Piranha began, "lives in a modest two-story, three-bedroom townhouse inside of Meyerland. You've been to Meyerland, I'm sure. Not too good, not too bad. Average. Suburban. Safe, but not too safe. Our cars are a Camry, an Odyssey and an old 1996 Eclipse—that one we have for almost ten years. I've got a wife who bakes weekly cookies for her church and a teenage daughter who gossips daily on her phone. Both of them know what I do."

Piranha paused. The hefty Asian man sitting across from him submitted a smirk.

"I don't like drugs," he continued. "They fuck people up, fuck families up, fuck communities up, but at the end of the day, it's a business that gives my family what it wants. The owner of McDonald's doesn't care about making America fatter. This current retarded president, George W., doesn't give a shit about sending kids to war. But you know what? It's business. We gotta do what we gotta do. I make this all work because I see it as that. And that's what you gotta do. You feel me?"

Pete nodded.

Piranha pointed at the stocky Asian man. "This is Andrew. He's going to be heading the operations in Alief, near Chinatown. You and Danny are going to follow him. I'm giving you a second chance, Pete. This is a business. Remember that. Don't fuck this shit up again."

"Ah, man. You know a nigga do, ain't nuthin' but growing pains. But now I'm a grown nigga, you best heard, my nigga," expressed Pete.

The drug baron winced.

"Why do you kids talk like that nowadays? Damn hip-hop," commented Piranha.

With that said, he dismissed the two of them. Pete headed outside past the bustling weekend crowd. It was an early March night, with the last traces of winter found upon the occasional breeze.

"Where to now, nigga?" asked his Cambodian companion.

"Shit, nigga. We back in the game, nigga," smiled Pete. "We celebratin'!"

———————

Cody made the usual call.

He had been phoning Daphne almost every night at fifteen minutes before ten o'clock. There was little advancement made, but the anticipation still gave his life a little flavor. It helped take away the disturbing memories of hitting someone with his car a couple of weeks back. The phone calls usually went unanswered for seven to eight rings before she'd pick up. Cody wondered if she did this on purpose or if her cell phone was left somewhere far from her during this time of night.

Finally, Daphne picked up.

"Hey," she answered.

"Hi, Daphne, it's me Cody," he replied.

"I know it's you, cell phones have caller ID."

"Yeah, sorry. So...how was your day?"

"Oh, you know. Work. Studying for my GMAT."

"And how's that coming along? Need any help?"

"How could you possibly help me, Cody?"

"I don't know. We could play study Monopoly. I usually do that. You could swap out the Community and Chance cards. Replace them with index cards that contain study questions. Have it where property can't be purchased without correctly answering the questions. Those are the rules."

"You're really weird, you know that?" said Daphne.

"I like to think outside the box."

"Why? It makes you strange. I prefer to study like a healthy normal person, Cody."

"Okay. I was just offering a suggestion."

"Yeah. Thanks."

There was a pause in their conversation.

"Hey," asked Cody, "why don't you come to my house some time? Let me cook for you."

"Nice try. No."

"What do you mean 'nice try?'"

"You're just trying to get into my pants. You'll have candles, I'll be trapped in your home, and you'll get my guard down with some wine."

"No, I won't. I thought we were friends. Friends can't invite each other to dinner?"

"It's not a very Christian thing. A guy and a girl can't be

alone together. Especially alone in a house."

"Okay, well, I make a killer shrimp scampi. That's too bad. What about a restaurant? We had lunch in public together. How about a restaurant for dinner?"

"It would have to be one where I would have zero chance of being seen with you," she said matter-of-factly.

Cody thought up of a list of places in his head.

"Cafe 101?" he suggested.

"Are you kidding me? That's the most popular Asian restaurant in Chinatown. I'll most likely bump into someone I know. Try again."

"How about, uh, um...do you like Italian?"

"No. I just had that."

"Oh, what about French then? I know a nice French restaurant near our homes. You live a few blocks from me, right?"

"Yeah, how'd you know?"

"I threw a Christmas party at my house a couple of months back and invited some people from church. You didn't come. Felix mentioned how close it was to your house and that you were a couple of blocks near me," explained Cody.

"I see. Felix has a big mouth," she observed.

"It's fine. I was just mentioning it because the restaurant is so close. We can get back to your house before ten o'clock, just the way you prefer."

"Yeah, okay. I guess," she paused. "Okay. It's almost ten. I'm hanging up now."

"What? There's six more minutes," Cody pleaded.

"Close enough."

"Well, when would you like to have dinner then?"

"I'll let you know."

"Will you be going to the church retreat in two weeks?"

"Yeah," she answered, "I'm one of the counselors."

"Oh. I'm going too. I'm bringing my cousin. Alright, is there anything you'd like for me to pray for?"

Daphne let out a judgmental laugh.

"Cody, how long have you been a Christian? How could you possibly know what to pray for?" she asked.

"It's the thought that counts, isn't it?"

"No, it's not. You don't know anything. If I wanted a prayer, I'd ask Luke or Ennis. And anyway, why do you always ask that? Do you think it would score points with me? Honestly."

"I've got little to say. I know nothing about you. You never tell me anything besides very small details, but even then, I don't know much about those things either. I don't know what your favorite color is, what kind of music you like, what types of movies you like to watch, who your best friends are outside of church, let alone anything about your family. All I know is that you're Daphne from church and that you drive a Volkswagen Passat."

"And why should you know any of those other things, Cody? We're just friends," Daphne replied.

"I'm just saying that we—"

"One more minute 'til ten o'clock," interrupted Daphne.

"Wait, wait. Before you hang up. Since you won't tell me much about you, I'll tell you something about me. I was born and raised in Houston, I'm a graphic designer and web developer, I like R&B, I have no siblings, my parents both live here, I like reading books and comics, I like cooking and dining out and my favorite color is black," described Cody.

"Okay," she said. He could picture her on the phone, glaring at an object that represented him. "That's nice to know. Alright, it's ten now. Bye."

Daphne immediately hung up.

———————

Cody slowly started waking up from his dream. It was the reoccurring one with the giant boulder rolling behind him as he ran down an endless, spiraling stairway. That was one of his two usual dreams. The other was an absurd dream where he was saving fish from drowning. He had never awakened screaming in any of them. Perhaps he was so used to it that he realized he was dreaming. Whenever it reached that point, Cody would turn around and stop running, letting the boulder pass through him, or, in the case of the second dream, returning the fish back to sea. This ending calmed him. It led him to wake up in a happier mood, knowing his worries were illusions. If only that were the case in reality, he sighed.

It was late Saturday morning.

As Cody rolled the other way to retrieve his glasses, he made out a human figure standing beside his bed, staring at him.

"Aaaahh!" he screamed, quickly putting on his glasses.

It was Mindy.

"Bubble!" she replied, "you scared me! You okay?! You have the nightmare?!"

"What are you doing standing here next to me in my bedroom?!"

"I wanted to see if you would have lunch with me. You are naked!"

"Where're my shorts?!"

"I see them in the other side of the room. Do you just take off your pants at night and throw them around? Hahaha!" laughed Mindy.

"Just hand them over to me," demanded a sensitive Cody, clinging on to his bed sheets tightly. "Please."

Mindy continued laughing and walked over to the opposite side of Cody's bedroom. She picked up his shorts and tossed them at him.

"Oooh. Calvin Klein!" she observed.

"Very funny. Now turn around!" demanded Cody as he started putting on his shorts.

"Why do you sleep naked? Ants may bite you!" Mindy said with her back turned. "Are you done? Can I see you now?"

"Yeah," he replied, getting out of his bed to look for a T-shirt to wear. "How did you get in here anyway?"

Mindy faced Cody, "You gave me your emergency key, remember?"

"Everyone has my fucking keys," muttered Cody.

"You say it is okay because you could be on vacation

and I can come feed your cat," explained Mindy.

"Well, I'm not on vacation. You can't just come in here anytime you want."

"Why not? We're friends. I even talk to you on the phone when I pee."

"Please don't tell me these things, Mindy."

"Ahahaha! You are my best friend! Ever since my twin sister in South Africa left me, Bobbie!"

"You...have a twin sister?"

"Yes," she grinned.

"Really?"

"No! I am joking! Hahahaha! I am an only child just like you!"

Cody continued looking for a T-shirt. He headed for his drawer.

"Do you exercise? You have a nice muscle! Can I touch?"

Cody gave her a weird look.

"Huh?" he asked, choosing his favorite blue T-shirt that read "Secret Asian Man."

"Come on, we're best friends!" She walked over and pinched his biceps.

"Whatever. I'm a skinny lightweight toothpick," muttered Cody, putting on the shirt.

The sound of a closing car door came from below, just outside the front door of his three-story townhouse.

"What was that? Did you bring someone with you?" Cody inquired with a worried expression.

Cody heard the front door open; loud footsteps soon followed. Someone was running up to the top floor.

"Yeah, I brought my husband!" Mindy beamed.

"WHAT?!" replied Cody.

A tall, middle-aged Taiwanese man with a giant potbelly walked into Cody's bedroom. He had a chubby face and a happy grin.

"<Why didn't you wait in the car?>" Mindy asked him in Taiwanese.

"<It was hot>," he replied back in their native tongue.

"Hi," Cody interrupted, "Welcome to my home."

"Hi! I'm I-Tsung's husband, Wing Wei!"

"I-Tsung?" asked Cody, looking at Mindy.

"That's my Taiwanese name, Bobbie! I-Tsung Cheung!" laughed Mindy.

"That...rhymes," observed Cody.

"Your name is Bobbie?" asked her husband.

"No, it's Cody. Your wife strangely calls me Bobbie all the time."

"Yeah!" smiled Mindy to Wing Wei, "because his head is giant. Like a bubble!"

"Oh! Bubble! Bubbie! Bobbie!" he laughed, getting the joke.

"AHAHAHAHAHAHAHAHAHAHAHA," they both laughed.

Cody did not find it amusing.

"Come on, Bobbie! Let's go to lunch! We need to talk about our business!"

The married couple waited in Cody's living room on the second floor while he took a bath, put on colored contacts, fixed his hair and selected an outfit. The entire process took half an hour. When Cody was ready, he saw them fiddling with his Playstation 2.

"Hey, how do you turn this on?" Mindy asked.

"The power button is right there," Cody explained, flicking the switch.

"Can we try a game?" she inquired.

"Yeah! I like game! Especially man game!" said Wing Wei.

"I only have 'man' games. This one is a fighting game," explained Cody.

Cody and Wing Wei played a round from a brand new video game named Tekken 5, which was one of Cody's favorite games. Since Cody was familiar with it, he allowed Wing Wei to beat his virtual character.

"Hahahaha! I want to play too, Bobbie!" demanded Mindy.

She grabbed his controller and chose a female character.

"She looks like me, huh?" she asked.

"Um, she's Brazilian," said Cody. "Nothing like you at

all."

The virtual match began. Mindy started mashing the controller's buttons, laughing maniacally while she virtually beat up her husband's fighter. Less than a minute later, she won the match.

"Ahahahahahaha! Man, this game is so fun, man! Maaaaan!!!" she shouted.

"Wanna play again?" offered Cody.

"No, one time is fun. Two times, too much. Let's go eat!" Mindy declared.

"Where do you want to go?" Cody asked.

"Cafe 101! That is where all the Asians go!" she smiled.

"Good Taiwanese food too!" exclaimed her husband.

The three of them rode in Wing Wei's SUV. Mindy sat in the back with Cody while her husband drove. During the ride, they discussed various topics including the idiocy of daylight savings, Chien-Ming Wang being the greatest pitcher of all time ("he will be great for the Yankees!" declared Wing Wei, "you watch!"), and Wing Wei's special hot pot sauce recipe.

Upon arrival in Houston's Chinatown, Cody once again marveled at how far the Asian community had come since his childhood days in the eighties. Back then, the original Chinatown was in downtown. It had failed for various reasons, including being placed near dangerous neighborhoods and the lack of a significant Chinese population. Its demise was not surprising. Several years later, however, a modern Chinese shopping center named Dynasty Mall had opened in a suburban area of the Alief district. It included a large Chinese community-oriented bank and what was then the largest dim sum restaurant as part of the mall. This facilitated a foundation for the second attempt at a Chinatown. Thanks to a spurt of population from Chinese and Vietnamese immigrants in the nineties, it soon became one of America's best looking Chinatowns seemingly overnight.

The most famous intersection in Chinatown was also one of Houston's deadliest—the converging points of Bellaire Road and Beltway 8 had attributed to many fatal accidents year after year. It certainly didn't help stifle the stereotype of Asians and their poor driving abilities. Wing Wei was quickly reminded of this when he dodged oncoming traffic, where most of the motorists were following their own rules.

"Crazy drivers!" he muttered, "Chinese people can't drive, you know. That's no lie."

"Man, Cody got into a car accident not too long ago, man! He ran over a Mexican!" blurted Mindy.

Cars everywhere honked at Wing Wei as he nudged his way toward Cafe 101. A tiny old Asian lady driving a pickup truck almost rammed into them. Wing Wei cursed her out. Because parking space was so scarce on Saturday afternoons, he decided to invent one of his own.

"<Are you sure you're supposed to park there?>" criticized Mindy. "<I don't think you can park there.>"

"<Who cares?> " Wing Wei muttered. "<Tow trucks can't get to it.>"

Cafe 101 was best known as a trendy, sexy restaurant. With its dark interiors and neon lights, the decor was reflective of a night club. The waitresses were mostly college-aged Asian women who dressed in seductive, skimpy outfits. Being a woman herself, Mindy didn't care about that. She loved the restaurant because of its food; it was similar to what was served in the food streets of her hometown, Taipei. When they arrived, the three of them were escorted to a table for four. Mindy held Cody's arm and sat next to him, across from her husband. She leaned her head on Cody's shoulder while flipping through the menu.

After they ordered beef tongues, spicy intestines, stir-fried noodles, squid balls and peppered chicken, Mindy brought out a series of pictures from her Mosiac Decor collection. Cody inspected each one of them carefully.

"My CPA has done all the paperwork," she explained. "You be sure to show up and sign them next week, then you help us make a website shopping cart, okay?"

"Who's your supplier?" asked Cody.

"A man," she replied.

"A man named...?"

"He is called Odie."

"Okay, so what does Odie get out of this?"

"Don't worry, we take care of it. You just put it into

your garage."

"Say what? Why isn't it in Odie's warehouse? This is shady."

"Man, you shady, man!"

"Where is he getting this stuff?"

"He is in charge of the shipping entry. He put them in box. In secret. Then he give them to us. For a fee."

"In other words, he steals this crap and then it's in my garage. My house becomes a crime scene," Cody deduced.

"Come on! No one's going to find out! Your garage is empty, man!" Mindy looked at Cody with a stern expression.

"No. I'm not doing it."

"Come on! Man, come on!"

"It's illegal, Mindy!"

"No, it's not! You won't get caught! I already thought it out, Bobbie! Please, please, please, Bobbie!"

"I don't need the money. I already have a good job."

She caressed his arm lightly. Wing Wei read a Taiwanese newspaper, seemingly in his own world.

"Don't you want to be your own boss?" she smiled. "Come on, I see how Ms. Rachel yell at you during work. I am studying for my PhD, but I really want to do this! Have our own business! My own business with my best friend, Cody Quan."

"No."

"Pleaseeeee?" She made a walking motion with her fingers on Cody's lap.

"No."

"Pleeaasssseeeeeeeee?"

"No, Mindy."

"Pleaaasseeeeeeeeeeeeeeeeeeee?"

Cody finally gave in.

"Okay. We'll try it."

"THANKS, BOBBIE!"

———

The silver Audi with tinted windows pulled over near the Whataburger parking lot at slightly past seven o'clock in the evening. A week had passed since Pete Mok had been employed again by the local drug lord, Piranha. During that time, Pete and his friend Danny spent the past six nights doing some blow and hitting the clubs with former acquaintances. Both had no qualms about being small-time drug dealers; they knew it paid well. But because Pete had botched his previous gig, he and his friend were reassigned to working under the tutelage of a man named Andrew Huynh.

Andrew was the well-dressed hefty Asian man from their initial meeting with Piranha. Pete and Danny knew little about him except that he was well-trusted by the kingpin. He had been well-dressed both the times that they had seen him, a sharp contrast to their baggy pants and loose T-shirts. Danny was skinny and scrawny, wearing a baseball cap at a forty-five degree angle that covered up the side of his face a bit. Pete was fairly tall, with a near-shaven head and an average body build. Both usually twitched because of heavy drug usage.

The tinted car window rolled down. Andrew was in the passenger seat. His driver was a stern-looking Asian man in his mid-forties. The radio in the car was set to 104.1 FM KRBE, a popular pop station in Houston.

"Get in the back," ordered Andrew.

Both of the young drug dealers got inside of the Audi. Once they were in, the driver headed toward their evening's destination.

"Man, I hate this station!" complained Danny. "Turn it to 97.9. Want something hard, nigga."

Both Andrew and the driver ignored his request. They were in an old area of Alief. Pete recognized the neighborhood. It reminded him of his childhood with his friends Cody and Duke. He was their lackey, helping them refill their water guns with boiling water, bringing them canned sodas, running bogus errands. Even then, Pete realized he was a tool. He blinked to return to his current reality. Alief had degenerated. The lack of street lights made the late March evening darker than it should have been.

"Say, dawg," Danny inquired, "I don't see why it has to

take four of us niggas to do this motherfuckin' deal, you know what I'm sayin'? We been down with this game for a long time, nigga. I don't see what you got to teach us or if Piranha ain't put enough trust for yo' ass to come babysittin' here. Know what I'm sayin'?"

"This isn't a drug deal," replied Andrew.

"What, nigga?" asked Danny.

The sedan slowly pulled into the front driveway of a shabby one-story house. It was among a row of similarly bedraggled dwellings. The look of the area was typical of an old neighborhood in Alief. Pete could hear dogs aggressively barking from everywhere. The driver automatically unlocked the backseat doors, indicating for both the new dealers to get out.

"Ask for a guy named Johnny," instructed Andrew. "Tell him it's time to pay. He owes us forty thousand dollars in coke money. We want to know what happened with it. You'll recognize Johnny as the guy wearing a cast."

"Why we gotta do this?" asked a worried Danny. "We ain't no enforcers."

"Piranha wants both of you to see that this isn't about fun and games. Now go. I'm not going to tell you again," Andrew replied.

Danny and Pete nervously got out of the car and walked toward the front door. The barking grew louder.

"Shit, I ain't never done it like this before, nigga," commented Pete.

"Yeah. The fuck we doin' here?" asked Danny.

A thin, middle-aged Asian man with a reversed V-shaped mustache opened the screen door.

"Ah, whatdoyouwant?" he asked.

"'Sup, my nigga. That nigga Johnny here?" Danny asked.

"Whothefuckareyou? YouVietChineseLaos? Whothefuckareyou?"

"What the hell matter what the fuck we are, nigga? Is that bitch Johnny here or not?" demanded Danny.

An Asian man with an arm cast appeared alongside the man who had opened the front door. He was holding a lit cigarette in the hand of his good arm.

"Yeah, I'm Johnny," he said. "What do you guys want?"

"We here for Piranha, nigga," replied Pete. "You owe 'em forty G in coke. We here to collect."

"Oh yeah? Tell him I'll have it by next month," replied Johnny.

"You said that last month," informed a voice behind Pete and Danny. It was Andrew; both he and the driver had gotten out of the car.

"Oh, shit," muttered Johnny. He flicked his cigarette toward the ground and stamped on it.

Andrew calmly made his way into the run-down house. A three-year-old girl was playing with an assortment of cars and dolls. A pregnant woman in her late twenties came out of the master bedroom, seeing Andrew and his men in their living room.

"Tell her to take the kid inside and close the door," Andrew ordered.

"Come on, Andrew," pleaded Johnny. "I got the coke. You don't have to do this."

"Well, where is it then? Three months, coke is gone, you've got no money to show for it. It's not apples and apples, Johnny."

The woman, wearing a frightened expression, quickly ushered the child inside the master bedroom and closed the door.

"I-I-I, my cousin has an addiction, he stole it, man! I'm getting the money back from family! I'm selling my car!" stumbled Johnny.

"That little beat-up piece of shit 1989 Camry? I'm surprised that thing still runs, Johnny. Can't be worth more than five hundred dollars in the market. You know we hate doing this sort of thing, don't you?" Andrew calmly explained.

"Please, please, please, mannnnn..." Johnny begged on bended knees.

"We gave you that broken arm last month, just to let you know how serious we were. We did that so you could still find a way to get us either the coke or money back. You remember what I said if you didn't take us seriously. We don't like doing this next thing, Johnny, you understand that, right? There's no profit in it."

"Heycomeonwegotthemoney," interrupted Johnny's companion.

"Shit, dude. This ain't your business, stick-thin nigga." Danny pushed Johnny's skinny friend aside.

Drops of sweat fell upon Johnny's forehead. He continued begging.

"Last chance," explained Andrew. He produced a gun and pointed it at Johnny's forehead.

"NO! NO!" came a shout. It was the pregnant woman. She had opened the bedroom door.

"Please don't kill me. Please don't kill me. Please don't kill me," begged Johnny. "I'll have it by next week. I swear."

"You know what?" asked Andrew. "I believe you."

He turned and shot the pregnant woman in the stomach, sending her collapsing unconsciously on the floor.

"NO!!!!!!!!!!!!!!!!!!!!!!!!!!!!!!!!!!!!!" screamed Johnny.

"I'll be back next week. If you don't pay us then, I'm killing your other kid," said Andrew.

Pete stood watching the scenario while his companions walked away. Danny nudged him to walk out.

"Come on, nigga," Danny said. "Don't be soft about this."

Pete slowly turned away, walking out of the house with Danny. The driver calmly started the silver Audi and pulled away from the home. Not long afterwards, an ambulance arrived to save the woman. She would survive, but her unborn child was dead upon arrival.

CHAPTER 7: GOD'S PERFECTION

Duke sized up the girls in the group and calculated who would be his prey. He wanted someone wholesome, Cantonese, submissive, educated and short in stature. The thought of knowing about God was of little interest to him; it wasn't why he had agreed to come to the church retreat. He was looking for a wife and it didn't take him long before a prospect caught his eye.

The target was Zoey Vu, one of the prettiest women of the newly renamed Fellowship Communion Baptist Church. Zoey was youthful looking, in her early twenties, tiny and petite. This late afternoon, she was wearing low-cut jean shorts, a revealing white tank top and an extra large pair of Chanel sunglasses. When Duke first spotted her, she was carrying three large plastic bags of groceries to one of the cabins. That was where the cooking was being done. She wasn't meant to be carrying them alone, however; her childhood friend and soul mate, Felix, had forgotten to help her after hearing about the Xbox 360 tournament in one of the front cabins.

"Let me help you with that," Duke offered.

"Oh! Thanks. I didn't see you coming!" exclaimed Zoey.

Duke didn't respond. He removed the grocery bags from her grasp, looking straightforward as he walked. It was important for him to maintain excellent posture and some semblance of masculine dignity. Zoey didn't respond either, still occupying her mind with Felix. Both Felix and she had grown up together in the heart of New York City's Chinatown. They had gone through plenty of good times and bad. When Felix moved to Houston, so did she. How could she leave him? He had been there for her when it counted, which was why Zoey carried such a deep and heartfelt love for her best friend. Once Duke and Zoey approached her designated cabin, she reached out her hand to reclaim the groceries.

"That one," she pointed at the cabin, "and I'll take those bags. Thanks."

"Why were you carrying these bags alone?" he asked.

"Oh, my friend just went and left me alone with them," she replied."Can you believe that? I bet he's playing Xbox 360 with his buddies."

"That's a shame. A man should never leave a woman to do all the work."

"I know! Although I wouldn't call Felix a man, he's more like a big kid," giggled Zoey.

"Is this Felix your boyfriend?"

"No. It's...complicated. He's my best friend. I love him. SO! Are you new to our church? A guest? I'm Zoey, by the way." She extended her hand to shake his.

Duke transferred the bags of groceries into one hand and gave her an unusually firm handshake with the other. He made sure not to smile.

"I'm Duke," he revealed.

"Ow!" moaned Zoey, "you've got a strong grip! Careful there...I'm fragile. Heh."

There was a moment of silence, then Duke let go of her hand.

"To answer your question, I'm here with my cousin Cody," Duke answered.

"Oh, yeah! Cody's a sweetheart. So you came here to share the Word and receive the love of Jesus Christ?"

"Yeah, sure," he shrugged.

A female voice from inside the cabin called out to Zoey.

"Zoey, is that you? Come in here quickly! I need you to help chop some tomatoes. And bring the sauce in here too." It was from Deena Ling, Marco's younger sister and also the head organizer of the church retreat.

"I gotta go," Zoey said, giving Duke a mischievous smile.

"Let me take these groceries inside for you," insisted Duke.

"No, guys aren't allowed. Not that I agree with it. Rules are rules, though. Give them to me, I got it. I may be tiny, but I'm stronger than I look," she replied, flexing her muscles.

"Are you sure?"

"Yeah, I got it. Maybe I'll see you tonight at the group dinner?" Zoey suggested.

"Of course."

With that said, Duke handed the grocery bags back to her and headed toward his own cabin. Inside, Zoey caught up with Deena and the other girls who volunteered to make the nightly dinner for the retreat. Daphne and Marion were preparing ingredients while Maple Washington, the pastor's teenage daughter, helped with the vegetables. Overall, they were making large amounts of spaghetti, ravioli, fish sticks, dumplings and pecan pie. They talked about various subjects including relationships, movies, shopping, cooking and clothes.

"Who were you talking with?" asked Deena.

"Oh, just some guy," dismissed Zoey.

Deena glimpsed through the kitchen window facing the street.

"You shouldn't be flirting with guys, Zoey," commented Deena. "It's not proper Christian behavior."

"I wasn't flirting with him!"

She started taking groceries out of the bags.

"You flirt with everyone, dear," Deena scoffed.

"Deena, how do I chop these onions?" asked Maple.

"Marion, show her how to do it."

Deena took pride in being bossy. Part of it was because she was a natural born leader, but there was a more practical reason. It also compensated for her lack of talent, beauty or wealth. She thrived on her keen intellect, claiming it was her natural gift from God. Deena liked Zoey, more than the others did anyway, but the poor girl seemed lost to her. It was in her opinion that while Zoey was Christian, she was also too easily tempted by the ways of the world.

"You know," Deena gossiped, "I hear one of the teenage girls is letting her boyfriend sleep over in her cabin. I told Pastor Lu about it and he put an end to that."

"Good job, Deena," Marion praised.

"Yeah," said Daphne.

Zoey gave a disagreeing expression, "And what's wrong with that? Doesn't mean they'll be doing anything."

"Oh, you wouldn't understand, would you, Zoey?" teased Deena.

The rest of the girls giggled.

"What do you mean I wouldn't understand?" Zoey asked.

Deena smirked, "Well, if you did, you wouldn't have had—"

"MOMMY!" interrupted a small three-year-old boy.

He ran over and hugged Zoey's legs.

"My point exactly," said Deena.

The child was Little Ryan, Zoey's pride and joy. It seemed to her that he always carried a bright smile. Although Zoey detested Little Ryan's father, she thought the best parts of him were reflected in the boy. To certain people, Ryan's existence was judged as a mistake, but Zoey believed God made no mistakes. After all, she reasoned, Little Ryan was her primary reason to live. He was angelic and well-behaved. A young single mother couldn't have asked for a better child.

"Why aren't you playing with the other kids, Ryan?" Zoey asked him.

"They pick on me," he replied.

"Oh, you know that's not true. Come on, don't be such a baby."

"I'm not being a baby!"

"Come on, girls," sighed Deena. "Everyone's going to be hungry. Looks like Ms. Mom here is going to be distracted while we pick up her slack."

"No, I'm almost done. I can wrap these dumplings up," Zoey insisted.

"Moooommmmmm. I need to pee. I can't pee alone," Ryan cried.

"Oh, my gosh, Zoey, just take him to potty already! Besides, you wrap these dumplings slower than a turtle," laughed Daphne.

"Yeah, shouldn't he know how to pee on his own by now?" teased Marion.

The rest of the girls laughed at Zoey.

"He's already damned potty-trained! He just can't reach the damned light switch! That's all!" Zoey angrily defended.

"Hey, no need to curse! Wow! Gotta pray on that one," laughed Deena.

"Among other things," added Daphne.

"Mommmm," pleaded Ryan.

Zoey picked him up and headed toward the bathroom. It was cramped for space, but far enough from the kitchen where the other girls were cooking. She didn't like what they implied about her and her son. Why did so many Christians forget to reserve judgment? she wondered. A makeshift stool was created from scattered telephone books for Little Ryan to reach and urinate into the toilet.

"Ryan, what did the other kids say to you?"

"They said I have no daddy," he replied. "Then they pushed me."

"That's not true. You see daddy all the time. Did you tell them that?"

"Yes. But they said you're in love with everybody else's daddy. That's why I have no daddy. That's why I'm a sin," he finished peeing.

A tear slowly streamed down Zoey's left eye, ruining part of her mascara. She wiped away the teardrop and helped Ryan pull up his pants, tightly hugging him with one hand while flushing the toilet with the other.

"Listen to me," she assured him, "you are not a sin."

"Then why are the other kids calling me that?"

"Because, baby, they don't recognize God's perfection."

———

It was past supper when they were separated into various fellowship groups based on age and gender. Both Cody and Duke joined the twenty-to-forty men's group, which was led by Ennis. The session was held near the lake due to the perfectly windless weather. It was also close to the basketball court where the guys hoped to slip in a few rounds of hoops afterwards.

They sat around in a circle, singing a few contemporary gospel songs while Luke played his guitar. Then Ennis closed his eyes and summoned Jesus, their Lord and Savior. When some of them had opened their eyes again, they saw Jesus among them. Cody felt an awe of amazement. He hadn't seen Jesus since his grandmother's miraculous recovery over a month ago.

"Wow! It's Jesus!" blurted Herman.

"Shhhhh!" hushed Felix.

Herman ignored him and started to sing, "You give and take away, You give and take away, my heart will choose to say, Lord, blessed be Your name!!!"

"Herman, shut up!" threatened an angry Marco.

Ennis took on a more calming tone.

"It's okay, Marco. We are here under the Lord's presence," said Ennis gently.

"Amen," the group said together, looking at Jesus.

"Who are they looking at?" whispered Duke. "I don't see anything."

"It's because you haven't been baptized," explained Cody.

"That's the stupidest thing I've ever heard."

What Cody didn't realize was that not all the baptized could see Jesus. One of them was Marco, who had been struggling to witness Jesus for years; it constantly made him frustrated and furious.

"Tonight," Ennis said in a gentle, accented voice, "we've all gathered here to discuss fellowship based on Acts 2:41 to 2:47. We are commanded to be together because we are infused with God's spirit. We know better than worldly people. We see past the illusions. We were chosen to save lives. That's why we're here; so that we can stay strong and keep holy. That's why we're having this retreat. It's what makes us different. As long as Christians stick together, we are infallible, you know? God Power, guys. God Power."

"God Power," they chanted in unison.

"Also," Ennis continued, "tonight we celebrate this fellowship by sharing with Jesus what we're thankful for. Because as Christians, we are free to love on a higher plane of existence. Anyone want to share some things that they're thankful for?"

There were a few seconds of silence. Finally, Ennis decided to speak up on the subject himself.

"I'll begin. I just...I just want to say that...I...I don't know...I love you, Jesus," Ennis paused, trying to continue. He started crying instead.

Felix patted Ennis on the back. Ennis sobbed louder.

"Whoa!" exclaimed Felix, "anyone else wanna give some thanks? I think Ennis has lost it!"

Ennis continued sobbing uncontrollably.

"I'll go next," stood Cody. "About a month ago, my grandma was on her deathbed. She had a very small chance of

living. My cousin Duke and I didn't know what to do. She raised both of us, after all. I prayed for Jesus to
heal her, and there Jesus was, right in front of me. He said 'okay' and she came back to full health. Thanks, Jesus."

Jesus gave him a thumbs up as he sat back down.

One by one, various members of the group gave a story of thanks. Herman told them about his amazing run for his audition in American Idol. Felix gave thanks for avoiding an accident at the most dangerous intersection in Chinatown. There were over twenty testimonials overall.

Ennis finally got himself back together again, "Anyone else? Please share your experiences with the Lord."

Jay stood up.

"Two years ago, I was going through some very hard times. I was about to take my own life. I came from an abusive father who hurt my mom. I was really addicted to porn. I felt things like homosexuality were right. But then, thanks to Ennis, you guys took me in and I found Jesus. Right now, I'm looking at Jesus and he's looking at me. And the light is there," testified Jay. "The light is there. My life has meaning."

After Jay's testimonial, Jesus got up and ascended toward the sky. Duke felt awkward watching many of them wave goodbye at nothing. Sheer lunacy, he thought.

"Before we say a final prayer of thanks tonight," said Luke, "I see that Cody has brought a guest."

"Yeah, everyone, this is my cousin Duke," introduced Cody.

"Hey, Duke!" smiled Luke. "Glad you could join us. Would you like to hear us share the Word with you about our Lord Jesus Christ?"

"Bullshit," Duke replied.

"Er, uh..."

"I don't believe in an invisible man in the sky. I think your beliefs are a reflection of your weakness. You use them as a crutch. I would prefer you stop peddling lies and be honest with yourselves."

He looked right into Luke's eyes, unleashing a primal stare. Luke avoided eye contact and decided to move on with the next topic.

"Okay, let's, uh, yeah, let's gather around," he said as everyone closed their eyes. "Ennis, would you like to say a prayer for us?"

There was a moment of silence before Ennis collected his thoughts.

"Dear Heavenly Father...we just...we just want to thank You...for being...I mean, Lord, You're just so great. So great. We just take You for granted all the time...and...I just want You to know...we can't ever repay You for dying for our sins...Lord...and I hope, I just hope, God...that...that we all keep receiving Your blessing...and...and that we stay true to what You want us to be and let us continue growing with You. In Jesus' name we pray, Amen," Ennis said.

"Amen," the group collectively responded.

Within seconds, the sound of a basketball bouncing could be heard.

The group of young men headed toward the court. Its condition was pristine, with bright lights and a metal fence that prevented the ball from rolling into the lake. Once again, they lined up to shoot free throws to determine who would play the first game. The first ten who made their shots would be qualified while the rest sat and watched. Cody knew better this time than to pick Jesus for a teammate. Eventually, they had selected their ten—shirts versus skins.

The shirtless team consisted of Ennis, Felix, Marco and two other members of the church. The team that kept their shirts on were five regular members who all happened to be white.

"Dang!" joked Felix. "Everyone else versus white guys! Or singles versus the non-singles!"

"That's not funny! Don't make that joke!" growled Marco.

Everyone else laughed.

It was two hours before their eleven o'clock curfew. The familiar sounds of pickup basketball were heard throughout the retreat area. With their fellowship over too, some of the girls came to cheer their boyfriends on. The first game went smoothly, exhibiting a competitive, yet cordial atmosphere. Halfway into it, however, one of the shirt players stole the ball from Marco, which resulted in Marco chasing and shoving him to the floor.

"Hey! What was that all about? I saw that! You pushed him!" yelled a teammate of the shoved player.

"No, I didn't! You're making things up!" responded Marco.

The shoved player got up and waved it off, "I'm fine, guys. It's okay, let's keep playing."

The basketball game resumed. Marco looked around. It seemed like everyone was laughing at him. On one possession he was wide open, but Felix didn't pass the ball to him. Why didn't he pass it? Marco wondered, was it because he didn't trust me? They never trust me! He felt a wave of anger sweeping inside of him. When the same opposing player he was guarding dribbled past him and scored, Marco felt disrespected. He deliberately ran at full speed and tripped the player, giving him a near ankle injury.

"Owwwww!" the opposing player hollered.

"What happened?" asked Felix.

"I dunno. I guess he fell," lied Marco.

"Yeah right, I saw you push him!" declared his teammate.

"No, I didn't. He tried to push me, and he missed. That's why he fell," Marco exclaimed.

"That doesn't even make sense."

"Stop fighting, please," pleaded Ennis.

Herman got up from the sidelines and started dancing randomly. Several of the others who weren't playing looked at one another in disbelief over Marco's blatant denial. Duke sat motionless, observing him.

"Come on, guys," reminded Ennis. "We're brothers in Christ, remember? We just talked about being God's children. We're infused by the Lord's wisdom. We're better than this. The game's almost over. Please don't fight, okay? God Power!"

"God Power!" they echoed.

The basketball game resumed with the race to twenty-one points coming toward an exciting conclusion.

"Nineteen to twenty, guys!" Felix announced as he

dribbled the ball forward.

"DON'T SAY THE SCORE OUT LOUD!" shouted Marco.

"Huh?" Felix was confused.

"WE CAN ALL COUNT. WHY DO YOU INSULT US BY SAYING THE SCORE OUT LOUD???"

"Okay, okay, man! I'm just making sure everyone knows."

Marco was boiling with anger. Everything seemed to be in slow motion to him. He hated the way Felix was dribbling the ball. He was dribbling it with his left hand, then with his right. Marco looked at some of the players on the opposing team. One of them was chewing gum. Another was coughing. This made Marco furious. He looked at the sidelines and saw Henry talking on his cell phone. Duke was looking right at him. Why is he looking at me? Marco wondered. Jay was pacing around. This annoyed Marco. Then he saw Herman on the sideline, where he was dancing and singing to himself.

Marco snapped.

"Let's get it started in here! Let's get it started in here—aaaAAHH!" Herman's singing was interrupted by Marco's tackle. Marco inexplicably pinned him to the ground and started beating him. Fortunately for Herman, several of the men immediately restrained Marco, pulling him away from Herman.

Ennis couldn't take it anymore.

"What's your problem, huh HUH HUH HUH?????!!" Ennis scolded, kicking the ground. "IT'S RUINED! THE RETREAT IS RUINED! OH MY GOD!!!"

He ran out of the fenced court, screaming in rage.

"Hey, what's Ennis doing?" inquired Henry, ending his cell phone call.

"FUCK SHIT DAMN ASSHOLE CUNT MOTHERDICK!!!" Ennis yelled, punching the door of a nearby parked car.

"Hey! That's my car, man! Stop!" pleaded the owner.

Ignoring him, Ennis jumped on top of the car and stomped on its hood repeatedly. He shouted more curse words like a man possessed. By now, most of the church members surrounded the car but were afraid of physically stopping him.

"Stop!" the car owner repeated. "Not my car!"

"DAMN ON SHIT IN ASS!!!!!" Ennis roared.

"Ennis! Come on, Ennis!" said Felix.

Finally, Ennis got tired and jumped off.

Luke reached out to him, "Ennis, are you o—"

"BITCHSONOFAHOLETITFUCKFUCKFUCK!!!" Ennis screamed, pushing his hand away.

He continued screaming away at the darkness, disappearing into the woods and presumably toward the cabins. His cursing could be heard from a distance.

"Let's call it a night," Luke concluded. "Sorry about your car, man."

"He was so nice to me the whole day," recalled the car owner. "Then he just changed."

"Hey, is everything alright?" asked one of the fellowship.

"Where's Marco? Weren't you one of the guys holding him?" asked Luke.

"Yeah, he's deceptively strong. He shook us aside and walked away, muttering to himself from here."

One by one, they eventually headed back toward the cabin area. Cody was the last to return. He took a long look at the large car dent created by Ennis. There were some slight blood stains because Ennis had been punching it too hard. To Cody, the bloody dent resembled a Rorschach blot. Regardless of how many times he looked at it, all he could see from the dent was Jesus' face, mockingly laughing at them.

"You're much happier than I thought you would be," observed Cody.

It was the next day. He and Duke were having an early lunch with the rest of the attendees in the main dining area. There were a total of over fifty people from various ages, ethnic backgrounds and gender.

Duke shrugged and offered a rare smile. "I just find all this chaos amusing. While you people brought me here to take a step closer to your world, you're all going to leave one step closer to mine."

Across from their table he spotted Zoey and the group of young women who had been teasing her. Women are different from men, Duke once lectured in his seminar. Biologically, the female gender is empowered by being a part of a collective group. The ones who are loners are weak and ripe for the picking. Duke envisioned the dining hall as a jungle with him as the lion. Soon, he thought, she will be his prey.

At Zoey's table, she was slowly annoying the church girls, particularly Daphne. She didn't approve of Zoey. She didn't approve of the way she dressed. Or the way she sat. Or the way she walked. She might as well be wearing a big scarlet "A" on her forehead, Daphne thought. Her history was well-known among the other girls. She came from a single mother, who also came from a single mother before her. And now she was a single mother herself. Zoey, concluded Daphne, was the rotten apple who hadn't fallen even an inch away from the tree. The girls sneered at her lack of education. While they had graduated from prestigious Texas universities like UT, A&M, Rice and Baylor, Zoey couldn't even handle community college. She had no significant talent and no significant achievements; all she seemed to be good at was sleeping with thugs.

"Maple, what happened to your arm?" asked Zoey.

Maple fell silent and looked at her new cast she had received that morning. It featured a decent collection of signatures and well-wishes. Though she was new to their church group and far younger, the girls genuinely accepted Maple with open arms. Being friends with the daughter of the pastor had its perks. They found out things behind-the-scenes and often got their suggestions implemented. Her connections with her dad were an asset to the group. Besides, they figured, she was pure Christian. Just like her father. Maple could be trusted.

"I was just trying to grab something last night," she explained to Zoey. "It was from one of the top shelves. I slipped from the ladder and busted my arm."

"But that doesn't look like the type of cast from a fall," Zoey observed.

"Like you would know. Are you a doctor?" giggled Deena.

"I didn't know they trained orthopedic surgeons at the University of Phoenix, Zoey," added Daphne.

The girls broke into laughter.

"Nooo, all I'm saying is that Felix once fell down and his cast wasn't like that," she clarified.

"Different brands of cast," Deena shrugged.

Zoey took out some Ruffles chips and started eating them.

"Ew, those aren't from Whole Foods," commented Deena.

"No, why? They were on sale for a dollar at Walmart," Zoey replied.

The girls snickered. They knew she had used food stamps to purchase them.

"Oh, nothing," smirked Deena.

"What's wrong with Ruffles? They're delicious," Zoey said.

"I guess. For your kind they are," Deena replied.

Zoey started to feel self-conscious and placed the bag of Ruffles on the side. She switched to the turkey sandwich she had received from the retreat.

Deena paused for a moment and cleared her throat.

"Well, Zoey, this is as good a time as any to tell you. We're not allowing Little Ryan to sleep in our cabin for the rest of the trip."

"What? Why not?!" Zoey asked defensively.

"He's a boy. He's male. He's not supposed to be staying with a cabin full of women. He was watching Marion change clothes last night," explained Deena.

"So? He watches me change all the time. For God's

sake, he's only three!"

"Are you going to argue with Scripture? 2 Timothy 2:22."

"Or Matthew 5:29," added Marion.

"Oh, why are we even bringing the Bible up? You don't even study it," expressed Deena. "At any rate, Ryan needs to stay with other men."

"You're talking about my little boy!"

"He can stay with Felix. You trust Felix, don't you? Heh. I'm not even quite sure that he isn't the father, if you know what I mean," Deena blurted.

Everyone within earshot gasped.

"How DARE you!" Zoey shouted.

Silence followed as the others anticipated Zoey's next response.

"Where's my son? Where's Ryan?" she demanded.

Felix rushed up to their table trying to figure out what had happened. Zoey's eyes watered.

"What's happening?" asked Felix. "Why are you crying?"

"Where's Ryan? Somebody please find him for me," Zoey said.

Luke took Ryan to her.

"Mommy, why are you crying?" he asked.

"We have to go now," Zoey said, packing things up. She quickly buttoned her son's coat.

"Why do we have to go?" he pleaded.

"Because we do. They don't want us here, sweetie," she said, fighting off tears.

"But I don't wanna go! I like it here!" cried Ryan.

Zoey picked her son up and headed out of the dining hall. Everyone was watching the scene unfold. She wished Felix would just follow her, but he was too busy arguing with Deena. She loved Felix with all her heart and it wasn't until now that she realized why Deena's statement made her so angry. It wasn't because she implied that Zoey was an easy sexual target; it was because deep down inside, she wished Felix really was the father. It hurt her that she could never have the man she wanted. She knew him too well. Once she was outside, Zoey made her way towards her car that was parked a half mile away.

"Stop," commanded a voice behind her.

Zoey turned around and faced Duke.

"What do you want?" she asked.

"The question is, what do YOU want? I see you leave here, all alone, a single mother with a child. You are in need of my protection," he replied.

Duke walked up to Zoey and grabbed her hand that wasn't holding her son.

"I can provide for you. I'm well-educated, well-financed, well-groomed. I am tall, physically above average and disciplined. Someone like you would be lucky to have someone like me. You are the type I'm looking for. I choose you," he said.

"And what are those things you're looking for?" inquired Zoey.

"Wholesome, Cantonese, submissive, educated.......short in stature. Someone who needs dominance," he listed.

Zoey let out a mocking laugh, "I'm Vietnamese. And I'm not most of those other things either."

"You may not be everything I'm looking for, but I'm willing to let a few things slide as long as there is submission. I see that you're in love with Felix, but let's be honest, what does he have that I don't?" He pulled her close to him. "You need a real man in your life."

"You got that right," Zoey replied.

"Time to ditch coach and fly first class."

Zoey's expression changed from a neutral to an angry one. Duke made a grave mistake by insulting the love of her life.

"Felix will have more class than you ever will," Zoey defended her friend. "You think I'm one of those fragile stuck-up 'Daddy Little Girl' types born with a silver spoon in her mouth, don't you? You're wrong. I'm from the hood of New York Chinatown, man. I've kicked and stabbed a few tough guys in the nuts who grabbed me just like how you're grabbing me now. And don't think I wouldn't recognize cheap pick-up tricks when they're done to me. Take your little alpha male gig elsewhere. I suggest with Deena."

She flung her arm free, staring back at him. She dared him with her eyes to make another forceful move.

Duke was taken aback by her sudden toughness. He was seldom wrong about his prey, but this opposing action of hers left him momentarily defensive. Zoey couldn't be taller than four-foot-eleven, he surmised, but here she was, establishing a position of supremacy.

Duke let go.

"I should've known you were a hood rat," he barked at her.

"I'm not a hood rat. I'm a single mother," Zoey said with pride. "And I've dealt with a lot of shit. Shit that you can't handle."

She turned around and walked away. Duke did not pursue.

"Mom, I didn't get to eat. I'm hungry," Little Ryan complained.

"How about McDonald's?" grinned Zoey.

"We're not going back?"

"No, mommy wasn't treated very nice here. We're going to find a different church. A church where people will treat mommy nicer."

And with that, Zoey strapped her son into the safety seat inside her 2001 Dodge Neon and drove away.

The lake at the retreat was a beautiful place to be on a cloudless, warm spring night. It was the second and last night of the weekend retreat. What had started out so promising ended up in a disaster. Numerous incidents of drama and disagreement had broken out. A few friendships were ruined. Several of the retreat's attendees took an early leave. Rather than go on with the activities, the planning committee decided to impose a strict ten o'clock curfew. All the members were asked to stay inside their cabins during lockout. Yet, two of them wondered, how can anyone waste a gorgeous March evening like this?

Hence, silhouettes of the clandestine duo made their way past the small patch of trees dividing the cabin area and the lake. The retreat was several hours from town, enough to be serenaded by the rhythmic orchestra of assorted chirping and croaking. The flawless reflection of the moon from the lake was even more beautiful than the moon itself.

"What a weekend, huh?" Luke asked.

"We tried our best. Guess there're a lot of things we need to work on. Maybe we should start with a smaller group next time," suggested Felix.

Luke gave a moment's pause.

"Just between us," the preacher's son began, "Marco really bothers me. I don't know what's wrong with him."

"Luke, he's almost thirty-five years old. He's never had a relationship."

"You really think that's it? He just lacks being loved?"

"What else could it be? He has a good job, a supportive family."

"I think he's bipolar," suggested Luke.

"Maybe."

"Even then, sometimes Deena needs to keep her brother in check. It's getting embarrassing. Did you know he yelled at one of the elementary school kids last Sunday? He accused the boy of taking the last carton of milk. But there were cartons everywhere. He almost attacked that child."

"He wasn't like that before, man. That's why I don't think he's bipolar," contemplated Felix.

Luke and Felix sat in brief silence looking at the lake and the moon. Finally, Felix spoke.

"You know, sometimes it's harder than we think to be alone. I hate what I'm putting Zoey through," Felix muttered.

"Don't feel guilty about that. It's not your fault. She understands."

"No, it's not that. She can never get enough credit, you

know? I get a lot of praise for taking care of her after the drama with her son's father, but she always protects me too and nobody knows it. She does it for me."

"Felix..."

"So it must be hard for Marco and Zoey. To be all alone. Unlike us..."

Felix leaned close to Luke. He felt safe in Luke's well-toned arms and pressed his ear next to Luke's chest to hear his gentle heart beating. As hard as it was for Felix to hide his secret, it must have been even more difficult for a pastor's ideal son to keep it from the world.

It was the perfect night for romance, one that was irresistible for even the most covert of lovers. Slowly, Felix lifted his lips and met Luke's. They kissed passionately under the midnight glow. The temporary feeling of freedom made them forget the past and future; it was only the moment that mattered.

"Mmmm...ahhh...oooh," moaned Luke.

"Huuuuhhhhh...ooooooh," smiled Felix.

From a distance, another pair of eyes was watching them. Jay Zhang had also snuck out his cabin to hike around the lake area. His cabin mate, Henry, had fallen asleep, but Jay was a night owl who couldn't stand being awake with little to do. He had not expected to see this private display of homosexuality between two prominent church members, both of whom he had grown to trust as brothers through fellowship. Felix and Luke continued to caress and kiss one another for twenty more minutes, but Jay had long left them by then, terrified with what he had seen.

CHAPTER 8: JUST FRIENDS

Cody couldn't remember the last time he had alcohol. Or intimacy. Or anything else that was fun, for that matter. He was beginning to have doubts about Christianity. Not the kind of doubt in regard to faith. It was the kind of doubt that was about dogma. He was still unclear of whether or not the modern concept of church was even mentioned in the Bible, let alone all the rules that were loose interpretations of the Ten Commandments. For example, he began to enjoy cursing again. Did saying the word "fuck" really equate to saying the Lord's name in vain? Did it lead people into thinking it was of less Christlike behavior? He wondered about that. And why must they be absolutely obedient to Pastor Lu and Pastor Washington anyway? Words like "flock" and "sheep" bothered Cody a great deal more than words like "shit" and "ass." Then there was also the genuine unhappiness surrounding most of the church members as well. The whole situation seemed like a clean room with dirt swept under the rug.

It was mid-April now. Although only two months had passed since his baptism, Cody had actually given his life for Christianity the prior year. He had been recruited by Ennis, his longtime friend since middle school, for a game of "church basketball." There, he had learned about religion as often as he played. He had sensed the church basketball group's ulterior motive was to convert him, but Cody wanted to be pursued. He loved the attention he received, and that was how he ultimately gave his heart to Jesus. It had made him feel accepted. He thought he had made friends.

Cody knew better now. He was still alone.

Physically at the moment, he wasn't. He was sitting around waiting for Daphne at a cozy sushi restaurant named Sasaki. It was one of those hidden gems where it looked modest and "invisible" from the outside, but pleasantly wonderful and authentic on the inside. It didn't feel like one of the trendy lounge "Japanese" restaurants that were rapidly spreading like a virus across contemporary America. Sasaki had the homely feel that kept things simple and didn't start naming their rolls based on city or states.

Psychologically, however, Cody did feel alone.

Once he had verbally committed to accepting Christ, the fellowship had moved on. It felt like a sales job. What Cody wanted more than anything was a deep friend. Perhaps, he realized, that was why he endured Daphne's consolation prize for friendship status. It was better than feeling lonely.

"Sorry I'm late. It's usually the other way around, isn't it?" asked Daphne.

She came in a jogging shirt and unflattering sweat pants. Her hair was unkempt and she didn't bother with even a trace of makeup. That was all Cody needed to know about how important he was to her. Conversely, he was dressed for the occasion. He didn't overdo it, but he did choose a decent dress shirt, had on colored contacts and fixed his hair.

"So what's the occasion?" she asked. "Why'd you invite me to dinner? You made it seem like it was an emergency."

"No emergency at all," Cody corrected. "Can't two friends go out for dinner?"

"Not together alone."

"What happened to being friends like Will and Grace?"

"Okay, what do you want? Do you need me to pray for you? Questions about Scripture? You could've gotten Ennis for that," she said, taking a menu being handed to her by the restaurant's staff. "Thank you."

"What would you like to drink, please?" asked the Japanese waitress in a polite Japanese accent.

"Ah, I dunno. Green tea," Daphne decided.

The waitress walked away, leaving them unbothered.

"Hey, I got something for you," Cody said. He took out a small wrapped object that was equivalent to the size of an engagement ring box.

"What's that? What's going on?" Daphne was cynical.

Cody placed the gift down and extended both his hands across the table.

"First, hold my hands," he instructed.

"Why?" she hesitated. "Cody, this is awkward."

She slowly placed her left hand on his, and her right one on his other hand.

Cody looked her in the eye. "Daphne, will you be my girlfriend?"

Daphne felt insulted, but she also felt flattered for the effort.

"Eh...no," she quickly replied.

She immediately let go of his hands as fast as she could. Was that it? she wondered, did this guy take me here just to ask me that?

"Okay, good. I knew you'd answer it like that. Now open this box," Cody said, handing it to her.

"Cody, this is weird. Please don't do anything to embarrass me."

"Just open it," he insisted.

The waitress came by with Daphne's green tea.

"Are you ready to order now?" the waitress smiled.

"No, please give us ten more minutes," Cody requested.

The waitress smiled and walked away.

"Cody, what's in that box? That better not be a ring," she said. "I'm serious. Take that thing back to whatever pawn shop you bought it from."

"It's not a ring," Cody insisted.

"Then what is it?"

"You'll find out once you open it."

"I'm not opening it until you tell me what it is, Cody."

"It's the reason I asked you to come here. It wasn't because I wanted to ask you to be my girlfriend. I knew you'd say no."

Daphne gave Cody a skeptical eye. She slowly reached out for the box and unwrapped it. It was a transparent plastic box with a piece of paper inside.

"What the heck?" Daphne muttered.

She opened the box and picked up the strip of paper.

"FRIENDSHIP," she read.

Cody smiled.

"Huh? I don't get it. We already are friends," Daphne replied.

"I just thought from this moment on, we could be real friends. You know, not 'friends in Christ' but real friends. You just rejected me. You made it official that my romantic aspirations are dead. So let's move on and get to know one another as human beings. What are you afraid of?" asked Cody.

Daphne glared at him in silence.

"I'm just a person, Daphne."

"You need to be taller and weigh at least a hundred and sixty pounds," she answered. "And you look like you're still in high school."

"So we can't be friends? Because I embarrass you when you're with me? This was never about Christian ideals, was it?"

"And your dad and mom are uneducated and your family is poor," she added.

"So?" Cody said, looking at her eyes.

"As a child of Christ, I deserve the best. Even my friends need to be ideal," she answered.

"I don't understand the logic here. I don't understand all this unnecessary hostility. I'm a child of Christ too," Cody said.

"You're an adopted child of Christ. And you should feel lucky."

The waitress interrupted their conversation by taking their orders. Cody ordered several of their finest sashimi. It was an assortment of ika, toro, unagi, hotategai, sabi, hamachi and, his favorite, sake (salmon). Daphne was disappointed about the absence of fried rolls. They did have plenty of tempura though. And she loved roe.

The rest of their conversation was composed of small

talk. The distance between them that Cody had hoped to
eliminate continued to exist; it may have even grown wider after
the dinner. He had done all that he could to break the barrier,
but it was up to her to make an effort. As long as she chose to
remain unapproachable, tonight was as far as they would get.
The question remained: Why wouldn't she give them a chance
to know one another? Was it merely attraction? Attraction,
according to research Cody had read, was not so much physical
beauty, but how looks complement one another. They were
both youthful looking and Asian, and had the same tone of
olive skin and similar facial features. Daphne, however, did not
feel the same way. It was curious to Cody as to why she viewed
him as the most hideous thing on Earth. Indeed, he was
noticing that he was getting a similar vibe from Asian-American
women throughout the city.

———————

        The phone calls came in the middle of the night. On
the third call Cody was finally awakened. This was not
surprising. He had taken a long time to fall asleep, but once he
had gone into Slumberland, it was difficult to wake him up.
When he finally heard the last call, he had to stumble
downstairs to the second floor where his home telephone was.
His naked body knocked around a few random objects in the
darkness, causing his cat, Toby, to flee for safety. Finally, he
reached the phone.
        "H-Hello?" he answered.
        There was crying on the other end.
        "Hello?" Cody repeated.
        "Sniff...sniff...sniff..."
        "Who's this?"
        "It's Daphne," she said.
        The reply stunned him for a moment.

"Are you there? Say something," Daphne demanded.

"Daphne, what's wrong?"

"I... " Daphne broke down and cried some more.

"Where are you? What's going on? Are you in danger?" asked Cody.

"I'm at home," she sniffled.

"You're scaring me," he said, "Was there a burglar?"

"No."

"Did you hurt yourself?"

"No."

"Then what is it?"

"..............It's my ex," she answered. "I went to his house today and...and...he totally ignored me. Then he brought home another girl. Then I just left. I feel like shit."

It was the first time Cody heard her curse. So there was another side to Daphne, he realized.

"You're not shit," he countered. "You're the opposite of that. You're the prettiest girl in church."

"No, I'm not. Zoey is. Every guy ogles her. Before she left anyway," Daphne sniffed. "Maybe I should be a slut like her."

"Hey, don't say that, Zoey's a good person."

"She's a shameless, un-Christian flirt, Cody!"

"But this isn't why you're crying, is it? This is about your ex."

"Right."

"What about me? You know I think the world about you. Every minute of every day, you're on my mind. You know that's no bullshitting. I enjoy being around you. You're special to me."

"No, I'm not, you like Zoey. You should date Zoey too. She's short like you and she's more of your type," she replied. "Every...every guy wants a...wants a flirty girl. They don't...they don't want a good girl...a good girl like me!"

"Hey, it's his loss, OK? If he can't recognize a great catch like you he doesn't deserve you. It's his loss, Daphne. Some people don't know what they've got."

"I know! It's like he wants trash! You should've seen this girl, Cody.

She was like Zoey...she was...she was... " Daphne lost herself in tears.

"Okay, okay. It's not the end of the world, sweetheart. Who is this guy? Tell me about him. I never knew you were seeing someone."

"He's someone I knew...since high school. We...saw each other off and on...in college. This was our......fifth time together......we never officially dated."

"Sounds like he considered you his backup plan."

Daphne sniffed.

"You should be no one's backup plan. You should be their number one priority," assured Cody.

Silence followed.

"You know what you just did?" Daphne asked.

"What?"

"You just made me smile."

Cody silently smiled in the darkness.

"Hello?" asked Daphne.

"No, nothing. I was just smiling too."

"Oh," Daphne paused, "I don't know why I'm so attached to him, Cody. I just wish he would just tell me to get out of his life forever."

"What do you see in him?"

"I dunno. I guess...I guess I just want to see him meet his potential to succeed. He's got such a good upbringing. He's so tall and athletic. Smart—"

"—white."

"Yeah. Dreamy eyes. Have you ever heard of this new show that just came out called *Prison Break*?"

"I've seen promos for it," mentioned Cody.

"I just love the main actor, Wentworth Miller. If I ever see him, I would...I would tell him to meet me at a hotel room," cooed Daphne.

"..."

"..."

"..."

"Cody, can you do something for me?"

"Sure, what is it?"

"Let's role-play. I'm going to hang up and call you

back," she said. "You pretend to be someone else."

"What do you mean?"

"Just stay near the phone."

"Okay."

Daphne hung up.

Cody hung up the phone too and sat next to it. Ten minutes went by. He felt silly sitting next to his phone in the dark, naked as a jaybird. He was about to head back upstairs when the phone rang.

"Hello?" he answered.

"Hi," Daphne replied, "Is this 911? I've got an emergency."

"What's your emergency?"

"I'm tied up in my bed.

"And what are you wearing while tied up to the bed?" grinned Cody.

"Don't be crass. That's not a very professional answer, Officer..."

"Miller. Wentworth Miller."

"Oh, in that case, I'm wearing a see-through nightie, navy blue to complement my black toe polish."

"That's nice and everything, but I'm afraid I can't help you."

"Why not, Wentworth?"

"Because I don't know where you live," laughed Cody.

"25061 Woodchase Drive."

Cody paused.

"Come over here, and free me," giggled Daphne.

"Are...are you serious?"

"Yes," she replied, "I am."

Daphne hung up the phone. Cody froze for a moment before realizing what he was being invited to. He quickly ran back upstairs and found some decent clothes to wear. Once again, Toby ran for cover, fearing for her life. The cat eyed Cody's actions curiously, wondering why her owner was heading out during this peculiar time of the night. Through constant observation, she knew this was an unusual circumstance.

The squealing of tires could be heard along the empty

lanes of Westheimer Road. Cody breezed his way through rows of green traffic lights, hoping the entire time he wouldn't suddenly hit another Mexican. The political incorrectness of the thought made him laugh. He didn't care. This was the night he had been waiting for. He opened up his Integra's sunroof, enjoying the wonderful air. The mid-April weather felt like summer already.

Once he had arrived in front of her townhouse, Cody quickly made short work of the gate and approached her front door. Before he could even knock, Daphne opened the door, wearing a worn-out, burnt-orange University of Texas T-shirt and sweatpants. It was hardly the transparent navy blue nightie she had described.

"Hey," said Cody.

"Hey," replied Daphne.

"You're not wearing a nightie."

"And you're not Wentworth Miller."

"Fair enough. Can I come in?"

"...........okay. Sure." She took a few steps back from the door.

Neither seemed to care they both had to go to work the next morning; things had gotten a little interesting. Daphne's one-bedroom townhouse was two stories, compact and surprisingly empty. Cody had expected stacks of Bibles everywhere with a giant cross in the middle of her living room. Instead, it turned out she was a minimalist. Even though she lived there for years, it seemed like she had just moved in.

"Don't you ever buy stuff?" laughed Cody.

"Haha! I know! Ironic, huh? I work in the Galleria and I don't ever shop!"

"See? This isn't so bad. A guy and a girl under the same roof. It's not a sin."

"I've had guys in here before," grinned Daphne.

"So it's all an act, eh? The goody-good church girl."

"No, I mean, I love Christ with all my heart, but..." Daphne paused. "Come over here."

Daphne directed Cody around the corner of her living room where a grand white piano was the centerpiece of attention.

"Wow!" exclaimed Cody.

"Do you play?"

"No, I was in marching band. That was it. First chair clarinet," Cody smiled.

"My mom made me take lessons since I was five years old."

"Oh?"

"She was very hard on me, but it was tough love, you know?"

"Can you play something now?" asked Cody.

"Are you kidding me? The neighbors would complain!"

"Oh. Of course. Duh."

"Cody...I'm sorry I said your family was poor. I don't know why I'm like that sometimes. I pray for it constantly. I'm aware of how stuck-up I am. I've been told by people about how I think I'm better than everyone," Daphne explained.

"It's okay. I see past that. I know you're a good soul."

She looked him in the eye for the first time and smiled.

"Aside from my grandma, I don't have any family here in the U.S. My parents spent every dime they had to support me. They demanded excellence. I've always been the good girl. The model child. It's hard for me to see anyone else who have lower success and acknowledge them as my equal."

"Is that why you're always against Zoey?" asked Cody.

"Sort of. I mean, I think she milks it. She completely changes around Felix. Do you ever notice this?"

"Yeah, what's the deal with those two anyway? Are they dating or not? Is Little Ryan really Felix's..."

"No, he's not Felix's kid. I don't know. They've got a weird friendship. I have no idea why," said Daphne. "I'm pretty sure Felix is still a virgin."

"Are you a virgin?"

Daphne glared at Cody for asking such a question.

"I'm sorry if I've overstepped my boundaries," Cody apologized.

"Of course, I am," she lied. "It's all about chastity, Cody."

"You had a different tone when we were role-playing."

"We were just playing, Cody. What are you saying?"

"Nothing. It's just...refreshing to know that you may have a wild side, I suppose."

They both paused. With the exception of the piano, the living room was close to empty. There was a small glass table used for dining and a couple of generic photos of random still objects. The entire home, thought Cody, lacked personality.

"You should come by this weekend," Daphne suggested.

"I'd love to," replied Cody.

"I have the whole Season 1 DVD collection of *Sex and the City*. Watch it with me. It's my favorite show. I also love *Nip/Tuck*."

Cody laughed.

"What's so funny?" she asked.

"It's just...I just thought you sit around all day reading the Bible."

"Haha. I...do that too."

"And then you watch *Nip/Tuck*?"

"Yes."

They both laughed.

"I hate my dad," Daphne admitted.

"Don't say that. He's your dad."

"He lives with my mom in China. Every time my mom and I would speak on the phone, she would tell me he beat her. He's handicapped, you know. He had an accident a long time ago, which prevents him from finding work. He takes his frustrations out on her by throwing stuff. It's hard for me to trust men. I...I hate men, sometimes. I don't know how Zoey does it," she said.

"Stop bringing her up. You talk about her quite a lot. Do you think she even thinks of you half as much as you think about her?" Cody countered. "Anyway, I'm sorry to hear about your dad doing that to your mom."

"It's okay. He's an asshole," Daphne said with conviction.

"Is that why you don't like Asian men?"

"Because they remind me of my father? Not sure. All I know is that I've never been attracted to one."

"My cousin Duke blames the media."

"Was Duke the guy you brought to the retreat last month?"

"That's the one."

"I don't like him. He scares me. He stares at people like a serial killer."

Sunlight was seeping through the windows; morning had come.

"Okay," Daphne said, "you have to go now. Sunrise."

She led Cody to the front door. When she opened it, the glare of the rising sun was blinding. Early morning joggers were everywhere. They looked at one another for a moment, not as lovers but like two very good friends.

"Thanks for coming. Have a good day at work," she smiled.

"You too."

Cody reached for a hug, but Daphne pushed him away.

"No, we can't do that. It's not godly."

"Okay. Didn't know. *Sex and the City* marathon viewing at your house this weekend?" asked Cody.

"Sure, can't wait," Daphne smiled.

CHAPTER 9: WILL AND GRACE

Cody had never been in an arms deal before. This wasn't an arms deal, of course, but if he were to imagine what one would be like, it would probably resemble the situation he was in this early June afternoon. At a back alleyway in the Harwin wholesale district, his parked car was facing another parked car. He could only guess who was in the other one. All he knew was that these persons were the carriers of some stolen decor merchandise from Taiwan.

"So how does this work?" he asked Mindy. "We all come out at the same time? I hope they don't expect us to have a briefcase of cash."

"You go. I stay," she instructed.

"What? But they're your 'friends.' Wouldn't it be better if you talked to them? We're partners in this remember?"

"No, no, no. You go. I stay here, man."

"Why do you have to stay?"

"Because I am shy."

Cody gave Mindy a confused look. Doors were heard opening and closing from the opposing car. Three middle-aged Asian men began to approach them.

"Come on!" insisted Cody. "Let's go together, I don't speak Taiwanese."

"No! You go! He speak good English, Bobbie," Mindy promised.

Cody got out of his car and walked over to them, aiming toward the one in the middle who appeared to be their leader.

"Hey, sorry, my partner's kinda shy. So where are you guys storing this stuff?" asked Cody.

"<Who are you? Where is the woman who said she would meet with us?"> asked the ringleader in Taiwanese.

Cody did not understand a word they said.

"Um, any of you speak English?" asked Cody.

"<Do you speak any Chinese?>"

"English anyone?"

"<You have a Chinese face, but you don't speak any of it. Why is that? >"

"I...don't think we're communicating," replied Cody.

Cody motioned for Mindy to get out of the car. She vigorously shook her head in rejection.

"Money, yes. Stuff, yes," explained the leader in broken English. "No money, no stuff."

"Woman in car," gestured Cody, "have money."

The three Taiwanese men talked amongst themselves. Cody stood and watched. Cody's cell phone rang. It was Mindy.

"What's going on, Bobbie? Did they bring the furniture or not?" she asked over the phone.

"First of all, it's not furniture. It's home decor. Secondly, none of them speak decent English. You need to come out here and talk with them," Cody demanded.

"Yes, they can speak English. I heard them," Mindy said.

"Where?" asked Cody.

"On Skype."

"You've only talked with them over the Internet?"

"Yes."

The ringleader gestured for Cody to hand over the phone. Cody complied.

"<Hey, is this a joke?>" he scolded her. "<Are you joking with us? Our time is valuable and we will not be wasting any more of it.>"

"<This is my associate, he knows what to do, just lead him to the merchandise and then I'll give you the check>," she answered.

"<Are you the same woman from Skype and the phone? Why can't you come out? We're only trusting you because you know our connection in Taipei>," the ringleader angrily replied.

"<He's okay. I trust him. I don't like being out in the summer sun. It tans my skin.>"

The ringleader turned around and shared her absurd answer with the other two Taiwanese men. "<Can you believe this princess? She doesn't want to come out because of a tan!>"

All three men laughed. The ringleader handed the mobile phone back to Cody.

"What'd you say to him? Why are they laughing at us?" asked a concerned Cody.

"Don't worry about that. I told them that they can trust you, Bobbie."

"And that's why they're laughing?!"

"No, just...come on. Just get the furniture, okay?"

"It's not fur—"

Mindy hung up.

"Ha ha. Women. Many trouble, eh?" The ringleader put a friendly arm around Cody's neck. "Come. We give stuff."

The four of them weaved their way around the labyrinth of warehouses and wholesale buildings until they came upon an unassuming closed storage garage. Taking out a small key from his pocket, the ringleader unlocked the keypad. He then slid the storage garage door upwards, revealing a stolen cache of sealed home decor merchandise.

"Use hand," motioned the ringleader, encouraging Cody to inspect a vase with his hands.

Not one to look like a fool, Cody attempted his best acting. He gently tapped the vase with his knuckles and squinted his eyes, attempting to give off the look of a counterfeit expert. He counted to fifteen before he turned around and nodded with approval.

"No more?" asked the surprised ringleader.

"Oh. Uh. Yeah, let's inspect a couple more," Cody replied.

This time he opened a box containing a picture frame. He continued the charade by holding it toward the sunlight, once again counting to fifteen inside his head. The three men chuckled at Cody. After probing a few more items, Cody gave his thumbs up approval.

"Okay? Good?" smiled the ringleader.

Cody smiled back, "Yeah, good."

The four men helped carry the boxes of merchandise to Cody's little Integra. It was surprisingly able to hold it all. Strutting towards the open window of the passenger side, the ringleader began making conversation with Mindy.

"<Okay, it's all loaded.>" He grinned. "<Do you have our check?">

"<Here>," Mindy said, handing him a check from her purse. Mindy found nothing appealing about his appearance. The man had oily skin, bad teeth and an overall dirty look.

"<Is that your husband?>" the ringleader asked, nodding toward Cody.

"<No>," replied Mindy with a serious expression. "<He is my bodyguard.>"

As he accepted the check, the ringleader observed Cody's clueless expression.

"<I don't think he's your bodyguard>," he smirked. "<Next time, you might have to write a bigger check. You're lucky we're nice.>"

The three Taiwanese men headed back toward their own car, laughing and slapping each other on their shoulders.

"What was that all about?" asked Cody. "What did you guys say to one another?"

"Just drive," instructed Mindy.

Cody started the engine and backed the car out. They were silent for a few minutes, reflecting on their first deal. Then he decided to break the silence.

"Why do you keep secrets from me?" asked Cody.

"It is not a secret! I did not know, okay?"

"You've never met that guy. You totally have never met that guy!"

"Hey, I don't want to do the big argue, okay? Let's listen to your CD," she said.

She popped in a random CD from Cody's collection. Mindy winced, finding the music unbearable.

"Man, what kind of singer is she?! She sound like she shout loud, man!"

"That's Mary J. Blige. She's expressing emotion. Her man just left her in this song. So she's got to find herself a better man," explained Cody.

"I don't like it! She is screaming!" criticized Mindy.

"Okay, fine, fine. I prepared for this." Cody ejected the CD and took out another. "I made this CD just for you. It's got all the crap you like. A whole collection."

Cody popped in the CD. Her eyes grew wider when she realized it was a song she liked.

"Oh, Norah Jones! Yes, Bobbie!" she smiled, turning up the volume.

"I also have that sissy thousand miles song in there too. Track six, I think," he said.

Mindy fiddled with the playlist, "Do you have—"

"YOU HAD A BAD DAY, YOU'RE TAKING ONE DOWN, YOU SING A SAD SONG JUST TO TURN IT AROUND," the stereo blared.

Mindy squealed with approval.

"I love you, Bobbie! You pay attention!"

"Yeah, yeah."

Though they didn't know it, some of the merchandise was already cracking from the slightest bumps of the ride. They were indeed counterfeit.

———

Within the crowded merchant markets in India, a shirtless young man is seen running away from his pursuers. He dodges moving carts, bystanders and other obstacles, hoping he can successfully escape before completely losing his breath. Amid a background of colorful tapestry of primary and secondary colors, he finally finds a narrow alleyway to make his escape. He uses whatever remaining energy he has left to make a permanent getaway. Unfortunately for him, the corridor leads to a wide dead-end area where the chasing men catch up and surround him.

The pursuers begin shouting for him to die with great fervor. The young man, however, raises a hand to demand silence. A unique beat begins to play. He suddenly breaks out into a hip-and-shoulder gyrating dance motion that perfectly fits within the soundtrack of techno and traditional Indian music. From out of the dead-end shadows, exotically dressed Indian women wearing silk saris and ghagra choli join him. Together, they bob their heads and skip around in unison, singing the main chorus of a modern Indian song.

"That's ludicrous!" blurted Cody.

Daphne had declared June as Bollywood month. Both she and Cody had been spending weeknights together, sharing her quirky obsession for the popular Indian musicals. She would pick the movie while he did the cooking at his home.

"They were about to kill him and then he just starts dancing? This isn't a movie. It's a Smooth Criminal video!" criticized Cody.

Daphne shrugged. "You need to add more salt into your French onion soup."

Though she had gotten comfortable with their friendship, their actions and arrangements reflected a continued enforcement of her strict Christian beliefs. They sat on opposite sides of the sofa, said grace before every meal and avoided any form of physical contact, hugging or otherwise.

Their usual routine consisted of movie watching, television shows, board games, and helping Daphne study for her GMAT test. He knew those activities were mundane, but being with her somehow circumvented that personal perception. Things did get interesting on a conversation scale. They spoke openly on many subjects, especially their experiences growing up Asian-American. They were the same race, but their genders gave them vastly different perspectives.

"Hey, what's that?" asked Daphne in disgust.

It was the first time she had seen Cody's cat, Toby. The

overweight gray tabby was usually introverted around visitors, but it appeared she finally deemed Daphne worthy enough to be touched.

"That's just my cat," reminded Cody. "I mentioned her to you before, remember?"

"She's so freaking fat. Shoo! Go away, you ugly thing!"

Toby stopped and glared at her. She was insulted by Daphne's rejection. The cat changed her mind, making her way to the stairs where she gazed at Daphne with unreserved judgment.

"She's just glaring at me. How rude!" said Daphne.

"Now you know how it feels," laughed Cody.

Daphne turned and glared at him, aggravated that he would take sides against her.

"Yeah?" she retorted. "Well, you know what? There's nothing in your house that suggests you have other girls coming here. I don't feel threatened. You need to make a girl feel competition. The only challenge I'm getting is from your cat!"

Cody scratched his head. "Well, isn't it better if you're the only one that mattered?"

"I guess. I dunno. I do, but I don't," Daphne answered cryptically. "Also, I just hate that you even have a cat. Can't you be like a real guy and get a dog?"

"One cat for a guy's alright. No one's ever criticized the Godfather or Dr. No for having a cat. Besides, isn't it more feminine when a guy has little girly dogs running around his house?"

Daphne loathed being disagreed with and chose to respond to him with silence. They didn't speak again until a particularly romantic scene in the movie that left her with a despairing sigh.

"Penny for your thoughts?" he asked.

"What? Sorry I was distracted."

"I said, 'Penny for your thoughts?'"

"My thoughts are only worth a penny? How low."

"Okay, a dollar for your thoughts then."

"Heh," she chuckled, "can you imagine someone being named Dollar? Makes them feel cheap. My mom almost named me Darcy. How retarded is that?"

Cody noticed she was trying to change the subject. He decided to cut to the chase.

"So what's going on in your mind right now? You're obviously sad," he asked.

"It's Deena. She just got a boyfriend."

"Nice."

"Not nice. How come God gives everyone boyfriends but me?"

"What do you mean? I asked you out numerous times..."

"I meant a real man, Cody," Daphne discounted. "Someone who knows how to take care of things. Someone ideal. Someone who's best for me that I deserve...I don't know. It's like God hates me. He wants me to feel miserable."

Cody frowned. They'd had this same conversation several times.

"We've been through this topic before. Maybe you're just too picky," he suggested. "Maybe...maybe what's best for you isn't what you think it is."

"It makes me lose faith in Him."

"Because you didn't get what you want? What do you pray for? Don't you worry about the homeless or orphans? What about sick people?"

"We're also told we get rewarded for our faith, Cody. There's a reason why certain people are chosen to be baptized. It's part of God's plan."

They both paused.

"You think it's all corrupted sometimes? The church, that is," asked Cody.

"It...crosses my mind," she answered.

"Yeah."

"Like, I'm sure you've seen that commercial with the bald guy and those third world country kids. You think that's real?" asked Daphne.

"Not likely."

Another pause. Daphne returned to her original thought.

"Deena's new boyfriend looks like Jesus," she laughed.

"Really?"

"Yeah, haha."

"MAYBE THAT'S WHY DEENA WENT FOR HIM!" they both said at once, breaking into laughter.

"Hey, what do you want to do this weekend?" asked Cody.

"I dunno. I was thinking about studying. The GMAT's important," she replied. "You can watch."

"Again?"

"What's the matter? I thought you liked helping me succeed."

"I...I do, it's just..."

"You're my friend right?"

"Why couldn't we, like, watch a movie in a theater or something? I know you have to study, but take a break, Daphne."

"I don't think that's a good idea.......I don't know. It would feel like a date."

"Then let's bring one of our friends. Like Ennis or Marion," he insisted. "Why do we always have to meet in secrecy?"

"The GMAT is so important. I don't know. I'll...I'll have to think about it."

Once ten o'clock came, Cody went through the usual routine of walking Daphne to her car. He stayed to watch her pull away from his driveway. As expected, she ignored his waves of goodbye and carried herself with an act of entitlement. The terms of their friendship were unfair. As long as he was nice to her, she was reluctant to show warmth to him.

———————

Skinny Grandma had represented mortality to the Quan family.

Although she had always been a frail woman, she received the "Skinny" moniker for a less obvious reason. During the Japanese-occupied China days, Cody's grandmother worked night and day, sheltering her fellow countrymen in underground tunnels. Her tireless dedication and persistency saved hundreds of lives, one of whom was a surviving American journalist who dubbed her the Chinese Harriet Tubman. The "Skinny" nickname, however, turned out to be the more popular choice. It led survivors to symbolically equate her thinness to a vigorous dedication.

The family found out just how true that nickname was after her miraculous recovery. Since her homecoming from the hospital a few months ago, Skinny Grandma exhibited an energy and metabolism unlike anyone else her age. She cooked large family meals by herself, played mahjong on a daily basis, walked for miles around her retirement home, and constantly desired to see her two favorite grandchildren: Cody and Duke.

"<Why isn't Min-Guang here?>" asked Skinny Grandma, referring to Cody by his Chinese name.

It was another weekly dinner with her only son and daughters, but the eighth straight week missed by Cody. Duke occasionally made it but usually didn't because he lived in Dallas.

"<He's with his friend. Again. So he says>," answered Mr. Quan in a disappointed and frustrated voice.

"<Are you sure it isn't because he's dating someone?>" teased Skinny Grandma.

"<Impossible. We would've known. We constantly check up on him. Every good Chinese child knows that he's supposed to report back to his parents for approval>," boasted Cody's father. "<After all, we know better. So we can ensure that he doesn't make mistakes. We approve of his friends too.>"

"<Girlfriend? Ha!>" dismissed Mei. "<How can your short, stupid son have a girlfriend before my perfect boy?>"

"<And what's so perfect about your son?"> challenged Cody's mother.

"<Which one graduated from UT? Who's taller? Who makes more money? Of course, girls are going to pick my son first! It's just a fact. I wish you could just accept it. I'm not

trying to argue with you>," Duke's mother said while chewing a bite of pork chop.

"<They're both good kids>," explained Skinny Grandma. "<It's just embarrassing to me that Min-Guang can't come to eat with his grandmother anymore. I also desire to see him get married and bring over a nice Hong Kong girlfriend for once. Have her make me some tea. Ask me how I'm doing. My health may be okay right now, but who knows how many years I have left?>"

Boiling anger rose inside of Mr. Quan. It was disheartening for him to know how much Cody displeased his grandmother. He wondered if it were too much to ask for a little obedience. His son had an easy life and a well-paying job. Certainly women would be flocking to him if he had made an effort to get one. How hard could it be for Cody to find a nice Cantonese girlfriend and bring her over for family dinner? When their visit was over, each attending family member politely bid their farewell to Skinny Grandma for the evening.

"<Don't worry, mother>," assured Aunt Mei. "<By the end of the year, my son will find himself the perfect fiancée. He'll make you proud.>"

Strolling around the parking lot of the retirement home, Cody's father felt the fates assigning a mission to him. It was to find his son a perfect wife. One calculated according to Chinese superstitions. He would match lucky numbers, harmonious elements and, most importantly, compatible Chinese zodiac signs.

"<Someone born from the Year of the Rooster>," he muttered.

"<Why are you suddenly smiling?>" inquired Cody's mother.

"<Because, it's up to us to find our son a wife!>"

"<Can you please stop doing that sort of thing? I know this is all about competition with your sister, but these are modern times. Even people in China don't even take this sort of thing seriously anymore. Let our son be.>"

It was pointless reasoning on her part; she knew her husband was too preoccupied with his scheming to listen to her. Skinny Grandma watched from her third-story window as her adult children searched for their cars in the parking lot. Though it was almost eight-thirty in the evening, the Texas summer sun stubbornly refused to set. It resulted in an enduring sunset, one that seemingly never ended. But inevitably night would occur, she reasoned, and after that, the morning after. The contrast between the sun's immortality and her lack thereof did not escape her notice. She was not jealous, however, because she accepted that a finite lifespan was preferable to a never-ending one. It was the sun that felt envy. People, Skinny Grandma believed, received the gift of reincarnation. Life after death. Death after life.

Getting ready for bedtime, she lit some incense to give thanks to Guan Yin, the goddess of compassion. Then she called it a night. Once she fell asleep, the figure of Jesus entered her bedroom. He looked at her for a moment before placing a hand over her head. In an instant, a shiver ran through her body. The perfect health she had enjoyed took a turn for the worse.

Cody's grandmother started dying.

Daphne came out of the movie theater with a grin on her face. It was near the end of June now, weeks after she and Cody talked about watching a movie together. Summer nights in Houston were hotter than most daytime temperatures in other cities. The heat, however, didn't bother either of the long-time Houstonians.

"That was an awesome movie!" she exclaimed.

"Yeah!" smiled Cody. "You know what made it so great? They took a popular comic book and gave it the indie touch. They resisted going the commercial route and stuck with a long-term goal in setting up a trilogy. This is going to change things for superhero movies."

"I'm glad you talked me into coming to the theater with you."

"Well, it's your birthday. I just didn't expect you to pick Batman."

"Why not? Just because I'm a girl?"

"No. Because you have shitty taste in movies."

They laughed.

"You really seem to like reviewing things, Cody. Maybe you should start a blog."

"A blog, eh? Isn't that something all the church people at Fellowship are getting into nowadays?" asked Cody.

"Yeah, but you know...they write about boring stuff," Daphne giggled.

Her body movements were noticeably different that evening. She twirled her hair while she talked and fiddled often with her jean pockets. Even her preferred degree of personal space extremity was momentarily absent.

"Okay, sure," considered Cody, "I'll start a blog."

"Well...it's almost ten o'clock..."

"Aw, really? Come on, I'm hungry. Let's go to IHOPs."

"It's 'IHOP,' Cody," she corrected. "There's no 's' in it."

"Alright, let's go to IHOP."

"Can't. I really shouldn't. I want to, but I shouldn't. It's ten. I need to get enough sleep for work tomorrow."

"No, hey, wait. At least...come on over with me to my car real quick," he insisted. "I've got your birthday present in the trunk."

Daphne followed him through the outdoor parking lot. Cody opened his car's trunk and produced a large box. It required both of his arms to carry, because of its sheer size and weight.

"Wow, what is it?" wondered Daphne.

"I don't think you should open it here," Cody advised while carrying the box to her car.

"Should I open it at my house?"

"Yeah, I think so."

She unlocked and opened the trunk of her Passat for Cody. The box fell gently in with a slight thud. They both sheepishly smiled at one another in silence. She hesitated for a moment, but then approached Cody and gave him a hug.

It was a long deserved one.

"You're the best friend a girl could ever have, Cody. I mean it," she said with a heartfelt confession.

She let go of him and headed toward the driver's side door. Cody stood and looked at her, feeling like he was lost in time and space. The engine of Daphne's Passat started.

"Well, aren't you going to move? I'm going to run over you, haha!" she shouted.

Cody snapped out of his trance and got out of the Passat's way. He waved goodbye to her, then got into his own car. Not long after he arrived home, the phone rang. It was Daphne.

"Hey," she said.

"Hey."

She giggled. Sounds of her unwrapping the present could be heard.

"This isn't just a big box with a piece of paper that says 'Friendship' in it, is it?" she joked.

"Haha. No," laughed Cody.

It took a minute for Daphne to entirely unwrap the large box. Once she used her car keys to cut through the thicker taping, she opened it and found it contained an assortment of smaller wrapped boxes.

"It's twenty-six presents," explained Cody. "One for every birthday of your life that I've missed."

A long silence followed. Daphne could be heard fighting tears through the phone.

"I'll never forget you, Cody Quan," Daphne whispered. "Not in a million years."

She offered a comment of delight with each opened present. Some were silly, some were expensive, some were handmade. Each carried a symbol of their time together. It took a total of forty-five minutes for her to open them all.

"Thanks for remembering my birthday," said Daphne. "No one ever does. When it's yours, I'm going to give you the best present ever. I'm going to throw you a party!"

"But mine's all the way in December."

"I know. But our friendship should last that long,

right?"

"Of course," said Cody, "Why wouldn't it?"

CHAPTER 10: HURRICANE

"BOBBIE, WAKE UP!" screamed Mindy.

Cody could hear her pounding on his bedroom door. He had long since learned to lock it even though he lived alone. On this early September morning, he was glad that he did.

"Come on! Come on! Come on!" she insisted.

"Okay, okay. What...what time is it? What's going on?"

Cody took a glance at his digital clock: 7:32 am. Too early, he thought. He quickly put on his glasses and searched for some clothes.

"Come on, Bobbie!"

After finally finding a decent T-shirt and shorts, he opened his door.

"WHAT?!" he demanded. "Why the hell are you in my house at seven-thirty in the morning? You know what? Give me my emergency keys back—"

"THIS IS AN EMERGENCY!" Mindy interrupted.

"What's the emergency?"

"Man, watch the news, man! There's a Category Four hurricane coming! The same size as Katrina!"

This was important news. The announcement of a hurricane coming so soon to Houston after Hurricane Katrina would cause major panic in the city. Everyone had seen what happened to New Orleans and they were not going to accept a similar fate.

"But I thought it was just a tropical storm," he muttered.

"No! It's big! Real big! They say it will destroy the city, man!"

"You're exaggerating."

"No, I am not!"

Cody went downstairs and turned on his television. Every major news channel, both local and national, was discussing the projected impact of the coming hurricane. The graphics of the meteorologist's radar screen showed it floating above the Gulf of Mexico. It was almost half the size of Texas. This was serious, he realized.

Mindy wasted no time in panicking. "Quick, you gotta pack! Call your family! Call your friends! Call—"

"OKAY OKAY! STOP TALKING, I CAN'T THINK!" shouted Cody.

A thought suddenly occurred to Mindy.

"Oh, my God, Bobbie! What do we do about the Mosiac Decor stuff? I paid a lot of money for them!"

"We're talking about a fucking hurricane here," Cody said, packing his Playstation 2. "We can only take what's important."

The media continued feeding them images. They saw Mayor Bill White explaining evacuation routes and ordering mandatory abandonment of the city. The hurricane's name flashed in big bold letters across the screen.

"Rita," read Cody.

Millions of thoughts raced through his head as he stuffed his car with clothes, personal belongings and food supplies. Meanwhile, Mindy was on her cell phone, yelling instructions to her husband in Taiwanese. It triggered Cody to make a call of his own. He wanted to make sure Daphne was safe. Her phone went unanswered.

"Hey.......hey!" Mindy interrupted his thoughts, "my husband says we need to get gas as quickly as possible. There are long lines in the gas stations."

Cody stared at his cell phone with a worried look.

"You're thinking about the Daphne girl?"

"Yeah," he replied, "she's not answering. I want to

check up on her."

"No, no! You can't do that! You must think of your family and best friend first!"

"God, where is she?" Cody wondered out loud to himself.

Mindy slapped him on the back of the head.

"HEY! PAY ATTENTION!" she demanded.

"STOP HITTING ME!"

"CHECK WITH YOUR FAMILY FIRST! NOT SOME STUPID GIRL, OKAY?"

Mindy gave him a stern look.

".......okay. You're right," Cody said.

They spent the next half hour looking for the cat. Toby had climbed on top of the kitchen cabinets and was meowing frightfully. Mindy grabbed a nearby broom and poked at the feline, trying unsuccessfully to get her to jump down. Cody did a better job at convincing Toby by squirting her with a spray bottle. With Cody's perfect catch, the cat was now safely in his arms, though she unkindly repaid him by shredding the top portion of his shirt.

"OW! AWHAA!!!" he hollered in pain, "damn cat!"

When blood immediately began to seep through his shirt, he shoved Toby into the portable cage, locking it tight. Mindy looked after her as Cody went upstairs for a fresh shirt. The cat squeezed her face against the bar doors, angrily looking for a way out. Moments later, Mindy heard his returning footsteps.

"Well, are you coming with us?" he asked.

"No, I need to go back to my husband and leave town with him. You take care, eh?"

"You should put tape on the windows of your house. That way, the glass won't shatter."

"There won't be anything left, Bobbie," she paused. "Let me take the decor products home."

"Leave them. I think they're fake anyway."

"How do you know they are fake?"

"Just look how easily they break!"

"I don't care, man! I paid for them!"

"Then be my guest and take them yourself!"

"You have to carry them to my car for me. I have small power. And my nails are still fresh."

Cody looked at her in disbelief.

"How. Do. You. Survive. In. This. World?" he asked.

"Man, come on, man!"

After he had spent twenty long minutes helping Mindy with the decor merchandise, he immediately made his way toward Daphne's neighborhood. Pandemonium was what he found. Most of the residents seemed to have heeded the early warnings and had left, but the remaining few fought, looted or did otherwise destructive behavior. Without disregard to danger, Cody walked past them and knocked repeatedly on Daphne's door. No response. Perhaps she had already left, he hoped.

He gave up after the fifth series of knocking. His motives for saving her were partially subconscious; it was a chance to play hero. More so, it meant rebelling against the Asian structure of "family first." Cody enjoyed the secrecy of their friendship because it was one of the rare things of his choosing. His car and home were picked by his parents. His job was given by a family friend. Daphne's friendship, however, was something he decided and earned. If Hurricane Rita turned out anywhere near as devastating as Hurricane Katrina, he didn't want to spend his last moments with his parents. That would be a typical epitaph for an Asian-American male: found dead hanging out with parents. But now that Daphne was nowhere to be found, his family-oriented inclinations kicked in. Guilt quickly followed.

"Shit," he concluded, "I can't just leave my mom and dad."

He weighed the cell phone in his hand, stalling for an opposing decision. The phone felt clunky and huge—like a metal cucumber in his pocket. Hopefully they'll make them smaller some day, he thought. When his pertinacious accountability for family remained, Cody gave in and dialed his mother's cell phone number. She immediately answered.

"<Where are you?!>" she shouted.

"<I'm right now checking come house to.>"

"<Your Chinese is getting worse and worse! What are you waiting for?! Hurry up and come over here so you can be

safe! We'll protect you!>"

It took only those words to remind Cody that he was a child. Whether he was twenty-seven or seventy-two years old, it didn't change. Something was programmed in him to obey and feel like property. Once his parents had him locked on, he struggled to diverge.

"<Okay. Come will I now,>" he said.

His mother responded with broken English, "You here come, ok? Mommy cook soup. Fix you. Good boy."

Cody immediately complied. Whatever opportunity he had about running away with Daphne subsided. Now it became a timeline of hiding out with his family, drinking fish head soup and eating leftover sausage buns. He accepted those would probably be his last memories. The usual twenty-minute trip took over two hours because of the evacuation. When he finally arrived, Cody saw Ace's station wagon parked outside the doorway. He was loading containers of gasoline into his trunk. Look at that, opined Cody, even my cousin has the sense to leave.

"<Hello, eh, fellow cousin! Eh, I'm about to evacuate>," Ace explained.

"Where are you going?" Cody asked him in English.

"<Eh, Dallas, maybe, ehhhh, what about you?>" he replied.

"<My parents where how come no follow?>"

"Sorry? Me no understanding you," answered Ace.

"Okay, you speak Chinese. I speak English, alright?"

"<Alright, ehhh. Your parents aren't leaving and I told them I would feel, eh, safer if I got out of town.>"

"Well, why are they just letting you go? Why are they forcing me to stay?"

"<I don't know. Maybe I'm not their son?">

"Do you have anywhere to go?"

"<Ehhh. Uh...ehh...no. I just thought I could sleep in my, eh, car.>"

The requisite to obey suddenly removed itself from Cody.

"Follow me," he said, "We'll go to my cousin Duke's house in Dallas."

"<Okay, cousin Cody.>"

With a newfound independence, Cody ventured into his parents' home. Upon taking a couple of steps in, he found a bowl of soup shoved in his face.

"You drink now!" his mother ordered in English.

"Mom, this isn't the time for soup!"

"Always time for soup! You drink now!"

Once again, he reverted to compliance.

"<Ah, there you are>," exclaimed his father as came down the stairs. He was holding armfuls of pinwheels and incense. "<You'll be safe here. I've isolated the entire house with maximum Chinese charm protection. The hurricane should bounce right off it like it was a force field.>"

"Dad, we're going to die if we stay here! All the pinwheels, incense and fish head soup isn't going to save us!"

"<Speak Chinese, son.>"

"<YOU TWO LEAVE NEED MUST NOW GO!>"

"<Things will be alright. It's just a hurricane>," shrugged his mother. "<Now, drink more soup.>"

"<Mom. Month to last came hurricane people die kill many. Okay?>"

"< Everything will be alright>," she repeated.

Cody felt frustrated that his parents were living inside their own bubble. Rather than heeding the news reports and meteorology, they were counting on ridiculous feng shui and other nonsense. He wondered why they often overreacted to meaningless things, yet calmly ignored actual danger. It was enough to push him to leave. If they didn't care about dying, he figured, why should he stay? Now there was just one more piece of business to check on: the safety of his grandparents.

"<Where grandma is?>" asked Cody.

"<Your grandparents are both alright>," his mother informed him. "<There's a mahjong tournament going on in Chinatown. People figured they could take advantage of this time off. In fact, Chinatown is busier than ever.>"

The defiant nature of the Asian community appalled Cody. Now he cared about only himself. It made the decision easy for him to turn and leave.

"<Where are you going?! You're staying with us! You're

a child! Ace can go, but you can't handle it!>" demanded Cody's mother. "<You come back here right now!>"

"Come on, Ace," Cody said, ignoring his mother. "Start your car and follow mine. We're heading for Dallas."

"<But, ehh, what about your parents?>"

"Didn't you hear them?" he scoffed. "They seemed okay with dying."

———

Cody was roused from a deep sleep, feeling cold pressurized water hitting his face. He had a second of disorientation before remembering what had happened. By cleverly eluding the stationary traffic the night before, he had successfully made it to Dallas in just under six hours.

"Wake up," ordered Duke, holding a recently used garden hose.

"You...damn it...you couldn't have just tapped me on the shoulder?" responded a wet Cody.

"This is my apartment and we go by my rules."

Duke had honored the obligation of sheltering his cousin and Ace, but he was none too pleased about their unannounced visit. He showed his spite by offering Ace the guest room and forced Cody to sleep in the garage with the animals.

He sprayed Cody again.

"Ah, fuck you, asshole! I'm not an animal! Stop spraying me, you dick!" Cody yelled.

"Why not?" chuckled Duke. "You're sleeping with them, aren't you?"

"I smell like a hobo. Can I please use your damn shower now? I've been stuck in my car and sleeping in your garage for the past twenty-four hours."

"No."

"Yeah? Stop me."

"If you don't like my rules, then feel free to stay at a motel. Oh, wait, those are all booked now because of you refugees, eh?" Duke let out a loud but unnatural laughter, "Hahaha! I like the sound of that. 'Refugees.'"

He continued being amused with himself as he walked outside. Moments later, a stretching Ace came through the door leading to the house.

"<Wow, ehh, what a great night's sleep," the teenager yawned. "<Your cousin has a great bed in his guest room! How was the sofa? Um, why do you smell like, ehh, the toilet?>"

"I slept in here," Cody stated, "with the pets."

"<Because you wanted to look after your cat, right?>"

"No, Duke made me sleep in here."

"<Why would he do that? Eh, he's pretty nice to me.>"

A loud honk interrupted their conversation. Duke forcefully drove his car into his garage, causing Cody to promptly move out of the way. With much amusement, Duke got out of his car laughing. He dangled a bag of food and gestured for them to make their way to the dining table. A collective sigh of relief came from Ace and Cody; neither had eaten for over a day.

"<This one's mine. And this one's yours, Ace>," Duke said, handing out the portions. There were none for Cody.

"Come on, Duke," he said with irritation. "Don't be a dick. Not now."

"<It's okay, cousin Cody. Have one of my egg rolls>," Ace offered.

"Don't give it to him," Duke commanded.

He gave Ace a primal stare. Ace hesitated and stopped.

"<Sorry, eh, Cody. Maybe you can, ehh, eat later on when we are volunteering.>"

"Volunteering?" Cody looked at Duke. "Where are we volunteering?"

"At a center for shelter. I signed us up. It would benefit you to serve society for once."

Cody's stomach began growling as he watched the two

of them eat with delightful expressions. Thoughts of robbing Duke for his General Tso's chicken floated in his mind. Or at least robbing the bastard up in his own apartment, contemplated Cody.

Once their meal was over, Duke drove them to the shelter. They passed by flatlands of grass and dirt, leading Cody to conclude that Dallas was a dull city. He made another attempt to call Daphne again, receiving the same unpropitious result: no answer.

"Can we listen to some music, please?" he suggested with an irritated tone. "I'm really tired of your National Public Radio."

Duke's silence served as a no.

"That is some boring shit," Cody added.

"You can learn a lot from National Public Radio. I find its information very useful, especially when it comes to tax deductions and maximizing your 401(k)," replied Duke.

Due to Duke's totalitarian decision, National Public Radio was the station of choice for the remainder of the trip. Thankfully for Cody, the volunteer shelter wasn't much farther. Once they had arrived, he made a brief observation of their surroundings. Most of the Katrina and Rita refugees were black, though enough scattered numbers of Hispanics and whites were there to make up the fabric of a mixed bag. He surmised that all of them shared the common bond of being poor. It also reminded him of something his father once said: In America, Asians were never seen in poverty. This was true in most cases, but Cody didn't subscribe to his father's theory of superiority over other minorities. After all, he had seen some of the worst ghettos in China. Perhaps, he thought, it was much more likely that the more meritorious ones from Asia were allowed to immigrate. Or at least those lucky enough to be connected to someone meritorious. That, and Asians tended to sweep their troubles into the shadows, keeping the rotten apples from public view.

The three of them were assigned the task of distributing donated clothes to the evacuees. In theory, the refugees—as Duke called them—were supposed to fill out forms and wait in line. That system was quickly dissolved once multitudes of them decided not to follow the rules.

"I said I wanted red shoes! These are orange-red!" shouted an ungrateful evacuee. She threw them back at Duke.

"They're shoes," Duke retorted. "Maybe if you weren't so used to receiving free things, you would appreciate what is given to you."

"WHAT?! What'd you say to me, Bruce Lee?! I'll fuck you up!" shouted the woman.

Security came and removed her from the line.

"Next!" ordered Duke.

"Yeah, eh, you got some toothpaste, man?" asked the following person.

"We only have Colgate."

"Okay. Nice! Also, man. I could use some T-shirts."

Duke's withdrew his attention for a moment to notice what Cody was doing. He was skipping the line and taking requests on his own.

"Hey, man, you listenin'?" the evacuee asked Duke. "You're zoned out!"

Duke ignored him and turned to Ace beside him, "<Take over for me.>"

Cody had found the structure too cumbersome and decided to take things into his own hands. It was more efficient to make a list and retrieve their needs at once. While many of the evacuees seemed to genuinely agree, Duke immensely disliked that they were breaking the rules. Not only were they there to prevent chaos, it was also a means to rule the masses and let them know who was in charge.

Without hesitation, he grabbed his cousin's list and crumpled it up.

"Hey! My list!"

"You're breaking rules," replied Duke. "Don't be a part of the problem or I'll find another solution. Get back to the table and take requests like you were told."

"That method's too slow," countered Cody.

"Yeah! It's too slow!" the evacuees echoed.

Duke stared them down.

"You will do as you're commanded, Cody Quan."

"Man, enough of your bullshit!" Cody replied, leaving

the area. "I'm gonna go eat some chili cheese nachos."

"We will have words about this later. Remember, you are staying in my apartment. I am your breadwinner," reminded Duke.

Cody dismissed him as he headed for the food court. He surmised his cousin's ego would be more tolerable after eliminating his hunger. Meanwhile, back in the volunteer booth, Duke sought out a head organizer.

"Find us a new volunteer," he demanded. "One of our lazy ones just left. We're down a person."

The head organizer followed his suggestion immediately, pleasing Duke in the process. He was once told that in life one could either be loved or respected. Never both. The choice was clear to Duke; love was highly overrated.

"Why, hello there," chimed a voice with southern belle charm.

He turned around and saw something he didn't expect. The voice belonged to a petite, diminutive pixie of a cowgirl. She had on a western-style hat, with two long pigtails flowing beneath it. The girl was everything one would expect from an old Western movie, except for the glaring fact that she was Asian.

"Y'all wanted a new volunteer, I heard," she said in a cute southern twang. "Is that right?"

"Yes, of course," Duke replied, immediately getting up to offer her his chair.

"Thanks!" she smiled, "Don't worry about teaching me, I've been here I reckon since seven in th' mornin'."

"I understand, but different booths have different functions. You still might need to be instructed."

"Nope. You'll see. I'm a quick learner."

The girl was headstrong and fiercely independent—Asian on the outside yet Deep South on the inside. He had never seen an Asian woman like her before, certainly not in Houston's Chinatown or from his college days. By all accounts, the spunky southern firecracker wasn't what he'd imagine to be his ideal type. Yet, there he was, feeling the magic of love at first sight.

"By the way, name's Annebelle," she introduced herself.

"Annebelle Wu."

Duke gave her a strong, yet assuring handshake.

"Duke Feng," he smiled.

"Is that plural for fang?" she joked.

"No, why would it be? The plural for fang is fangs," he said, confused.

"It was a joke. I'm giving you sass," she smiled.

Duke tried his best to laugh like a normal person.

Concurrently, on the other side of the shelter, Cody was sitting in the food court, enjoying a plate of chili cheese nachos and chicken fried steak. Ace came over to him and snacked on some nachos.

"Hey, aren't you supposed to be helping out?" asked Cody.

"<Eh, a new person came and helped. I can take a break.>"

Cody took interest in the television showing the local news. It suddenly occurred to him that he had forgotten his own family the entire time. A wave of fear brushed over him. Today was supposed to be the day Hurricane Rita made landfall in Houston.

"<Hey, eh, how come the weather, eh, looks so nice in Houston?>" asked Ace.

He was right, observed Cody. The live footage from Houston showed sunshine and blue skies. It also switched to a clear picture of Galveston Island, showing happy pedestrians waving in the background.

"Son of a bitch," muttered Cody, "it didn't hit."

Daphne distanced herself from her coworkers at the tacky Las Vegas airport bar. She was tired of their gossip, mostly because she had no drama of her own to contribute. She was counting every hour, every minute and every second for their business trip to mercifully end. It wasn't like she had passion for what she did either. The world of finance was so dreary and dull—its people so focused on money. What she wanted was adventure.

That was what made the entire trip to Las Vegas so disappointing. She cursed Jesus again for not giving her that perfect boyfriend. It was the ideal setting. She imagined a charming rogue playboy in a casino, whisking her off her feet. They would do daring things, perhaps a secret society of witty and handsome thieves involving her in an elaborate but zany plan to rob the Bellagio or Caesar's Palace. Like Ocean's Eleven. Daphne sighed, reminiscing that fantasy. It was far better than her current reality of eating peanuts and watching news clips of Hurricane Rita. She knew she should have worried a bit more about Cody, but he was probably safe.

"Anything for you?" asked the bartender.

"No, I'm fine," she replied.

"Sure? Not even a glass of water? Those peanuts can make you awfully thirsty."

"Alright," sighed Daphne, "I'll have a glass of milk then."

The bartender gave her an odd glance, then complied anyway. He couldn't remember the last time anyone ordered milk.

"Gin and tonic," ordered a new voice, "and a Washington apple for the lady."

She frowned when the incoming stranger wasn't handsome and white. He was a hefty-looking Asian man, one she correctly guessed to be in his early forties. She gave him points for being well-dressed, however. The dark gray blazer that matched his black vest, white-collared shirt, emerald tie and black slacks weren't cheap.

"Where are you heading to?" the man asked.

"Houston."

"I'm from there too. What's a beautiful woman like yourself doing alone in a bar?"

"I'm sorry, you should stop. I only date white guys."

The hefty man chuckled.

"Here you go," the bartender said, placing their

respective drinks in front of them. "Gin and tonic, sir. Washington apple for the lady. And her milk too."

"Cheers," the stranger offered as a toast.

Daphne stayed put, glaring at him. He toasted her glass that was sitting on the table instead.

"You should try that, see if you like it," he insisted.

"I won't."

"Why not?"

"Cause I know I won't."

"You're religious or just an uppity bitch?"

Daphne didn't reply. She felt no attraction for him.

"What are you afraid of, Ms. Goody Two-Shoes?" he asked, "It's just a drink."

She felt that there was something dangerous about him. Not the charming type she was used to in movies or television shows, either. He carried himself with indifference and an unusual calmness, as though he could turn emotions on and off like a faucet. But there was something greater than that which bothered her more, Daphne realized. His entire presence mocked everything she believed in. He reminded her of how boring she was. She decided to defy him by doing exactly what he wanted. Picking up the glass of the Washington apple, she made the drink disappear in three large gulps, slamming the empty glass down with a resounding bang.

"Is that goody two-shoes enough for you?" she mocked with a naughty smirk.

"What did you think of it?"

She shrugged, "It was okay."

Her face was red and hot; she could feel her heart rapidly trying to free itself from her chest.

"You don't drink often, do you?" the man teased.

"I do," she lied. "I drink with my friends all the time."

"Oh, yeah?"

"Yeah," she gleamed, "all the time."

"So what are you doing here in Vegas? You know there was a hurricane in Houston, right?"

"Duh. It's just all over the news and everything. Heard it was a false alarm."

"Oh, it hit somewhere. Probably the countryside.

Houston got lucky."

"So what are you doing in Vegas?" she wondered.

"Business."

"What.......kind of business?"

The man paused for a moment. "I own a company that makes identification tags."

"Wow, a big shot CEO, eh?"

"You can say that. Another drink?"

"I...um...no. No, I got to go. My flight is almost ready," she insisted. "Are we on the same plane?"

"No, I'm heading to Phoenix."

"I thought you said you live in Houston?"

"I do. But I have business to attend to in Phoenix, first."

"Oh," Daphne replied, somewhat disappointed, "well, I've got to go now. Bye."

The hefty gentleman took out a business card from his wallet. "Call me."

Daphne read the card, "Andrew Huynh, eh?"

"Yeah."

"Don't you want to know my name?"

"No, we'll talk again. I'm sure of it."

"Yeah, right," she mumbled.

Daphne left the bar, returning back to her coworkers.

———

Sometimes Maple Washington hated what she was: short, stocky and geeky. It was cruel, she supposed, that she was part of a community that celebrated athleticism over academics. At least it seemed that way in southwest Houston, whose African-American community spotlighted the women's dominance in sports. It made someone so extraordinary like her seem ordinary. She hid her writing and art abilities not so much out of shyness, but because she was afraid that no one would care and understand. To a creative talent, apathy was worse than death.

That was why she favored herself a proud Pisces. Her father discouraged her from astrology, but it didn't make her sign any less true. She liked it best when her head was in the clouds, conjuring up ideas and scenarios for her secretly drawn manga series. Her constant daydreaming, of course, was also the culprit for her average grades. Maple supposed she could make more A's if she put her mind to it, but studying was so mundane. Lord knows her existence was lonely enough, she figured.

Things became a little less solitary when her father became co-pastor of Fellowship Communion Baptist Church. What she could hardly find in the black community, she found in abundance in the new Asian one. There were nerds galore, teens her age who were fluent in Yu-Gi-Oh! and Fullmetal Alchemist. She found girls who crushed on Bi Rain and knew the Korean lyrics to BoA's Girls on Top.

It was not surprising, then, that she had developed a best friend from the church in Jay Zheng. Jay might have been ten years older than her, but he was one of the first ones who reached out. Even though everyone was Christian at their church, Maple could tell there was hesitance for the Asian and black members to get along. Jay, however, had no reservations about talking with her when the church merging first started. She figured it was probably her No Face from Spirited Away earrings or her doodles of Itachi Uchiha from the Naruto series. Those were all the icebreakers they needed to develop a trusting friendship. It was because of it that Maple decided she would choose Jay to reveal her secret.

Her email took no longer than a minute to write; the video file required just a few seconds more to attach. She exhaled after clicking the Send button, knowing a big weight had been lifted from her young shoulders. The secret she had sent would cease being one by tomorrow. It was something that everyone in their church needed to know. Nothing would be the same again.

Five hours later, just after midnight, Jay returned home and opened the email and its attachment. What he read shocked

him; what he saw from the video horrified him. The time stamp
in the video suggested that it was made at the time of their
spring retreat. Its background featured Maple's cabin. The clip
started out innocently enough, but things soon escalated when
Maple walked past the door, beaten and bruised. Pastor
Washington followed, hitting her repeatedly with his belt. The
abuse stopped only after he had grabbed and broken her arm.
The pastor's expression changed after he realized what he had
done. He looked around for witnesses, believing there were
none. What he didn't see was the laptop camera recording the
assault.

The email read:

Oct. 3, 2005 -

dear jay,
i know we haven't talked much in church and know each other 4
long.
but u r a good friend 2 me. i know we r around 10 years apart, but i feel
like ur the one i trust the most. i need 2 tell u my secret. 4 the past 3 years,
my father has been beating me up and abusing me. remember my cast? i
lied 2 y'all. i didn't fall. it was bcz of him. he is a fraud. he continues 2 hit
me. mom knows about it, but is on his side. please send the video 2 the rite
people. i trust u.

ur friend,
maple

CHAPTER 11: JESUS STRIKES

Usually, Skinny Grandma didn't like nursing homes. They were a big contrast to the mirthful nature of retirement homes, which celebrated life instead of foreshadowing death. It had taken some time for her to get used to the hospital beds and the withering "residents." The loud, unified ticking of the clocks certainly didn't help, either. After several months of it, though, it had evolved into a tolerable experience. The one constant happiness she found was television shows. She had never watched so much American TV before, but she was a fan now, particularly enjoying *The Price Is Right* and *Wheel of Fortune.* Their rules were a bit foggy to her, though it was fun screaming "Come on Down!" or "Big Money!" She also found Bob Barker irresistibly charming.

The other constant was her elderly Hispanic roommate, the one she dubbed "the Mexican lady." Through hand gestures and the simplest of English, they were able to concoct an amenable acquaintanceship. It was all Skinny Grandma could do to decipher the basic details about her: eighty-four years old, two adult daughters and a late husband who passed away seven

years ago. The woman's name was unpronounceable by her
Chinese tongue. She figured it was something like "Ianamoosa"
or "Ismasala"; it was easier just to wave or call out "wai," the
Cantonese equivalent to "hey." Only one of the Mexican lady's
grown daughters visited her often. The other, she had seen only
once. Some nights, the woman would cry, though Skinny
Grandma didn't console her. She figured it wouldn't make a
difference.

By now, she had accepted the finality of her life; more
so, she was sick of its drama. Life or death, she wished fate
would make up its mind. Being confined to a nursing home bed
wasn't living. If anything, she cherished the serenity of isolation,
especially sleeping. She wished her own adult children would
understand that; their visitations and overworrying, frankly,
annoyed her. It seemed they were more afraid of death than she
was, making her wonder why the ones who weren't dying feared
death the most.

She couldn't stand their theater of sympathy. Had her
son and daughters come for genuine conversation, their
stopovers would have been met with more anticipation. Instead,
Min-Lo and Mei held suffering contests, masquerading as tragic
people who couldn't bear life's final curtain call. What did they
know about suffering? she thought. Skinny Grandma had
known real torment in her youth. There were hundreds of times
during the war when she could have been shot, raped, starved,
stabbed, beaten or drowned. Life had been a blessing for her.
An extended life should be celebrated, not pitied.

"<She's sleeping>," informed Aunt Mei.

Cody's father had entered the hospital room with a
large thermos filled with congee. He knew how much Skinny
Grandma hated the nursing home's food.

"<How'd you get here before me? You don't get off
work until six. Today's my day off and it's only six-fifteen!">
cried Mr. Quan.

"<Well, maybe it's because I love her more. You can take your congee back home. I already fed her and I made extras",> she boasted. "<Poor me, how I have to do all that AND work. It's so hard. But I got to do it. I have no choice.>"

"<Hey, this congee took a lot of effort on my part too!>"

"<You didn't suffer as much as I did.>"

"<That's what you think. I've built up a lot of karma points!>"

"<Just go back home, little brother. I've got this handled.>"

Their bickering woke Skinny Grandma up. She was weak with low amounts of energy. It was enough to let out a cough.

"<MOTHER!>" they both shouted.

"<I swear>," she muttered, "<the two of you haven't changed. Six or sixty years old. It doesn't matter. Still children.>"

"<Oh, mother! The doctor says you'll be alright, mother! He says you're improving!!!>" beamed Aunt Mei, nudging her brother.

"<Oh, yes. Yes! In fact, he says you seem more like a visitor than a patient!>" Cody's father grinned.

"<I don't like liars. I raised you better than to be liars>," scowled Skinny Grandma. "<My time is short. Whatever made me heal suddenly made me sick. But I've always decided to be thankful. Remember, the only thing you can control in this life is your attitude. I don't need pity—>"

Aunt Mei jumped in, "<Not pity, mother. I thank you—>"

"<—nor your thankfulness. I hate being old. I can't wait for the next life. So be happy for me when I'm gone.>"

The passion from her speech exhausted her. Cody's grandmother did little to resist sleeping again. She spent her last remaining moments dreaming. It was ironic how most people imagined their last hours awake in a hospital bed when they were more likely to pass away in their sleep. Knowing it was the end, she was thankful to be spending it in her subconscious where she was able to fantasize for a final time. She was a young woman again, running in a field among daisies and dandelions. Everything was perfect and peaceful, free from pain and suffering. There was no rush to leave, but she wanted to eventually. Perhaps just a little longer.

Hours after everyone had left, deep in the middle of the night, her heartbeat came to a conclusive, eternal stop.

———————

The routine had lost its luster by now. In fact, it had turned frustrating.

Cody punched the dashboard of his car as the White Sox scored another run against his hometown Astros in Houston's first ever World Series game. It made him furious that he couldn't watch his team play. Like so many of these kind of nights, Mindy had sent him alone on a last-minute supply run. Their company was making decent money, but garnering stolen goods at odd times in strange places had worn thin. He couldn't even remember the last time she had gone with him. True, it was dangerous work and Mindy wouldn't be of much help, but it was the principle of it, he thought. Besides, he was tired of her inconsiderate nature. He figured, at the very least, she should schedule the meetings better. Sometimes the locations would be in the Harwin warehouses, other times it was near the Houston Ship Channel. Once, it was even in the Third Ward. Tonight, it was in a nondescript warehouse near downtown. All of the meetings were held in the evenings where trouble was most imminent. After the last out of the baseball game was made, Cody angrily turned the radio off and sat in silence.

"Shit," he muttered.

Suddenly, he heard another car arrive pull up across from his. As per usual practice, it kept its lights off, but flashed them twice to signify its purpose. Its door opening and closing could be heard. Cody could barely make out the approaching silhouette against the night sky. Cody got out of his car and met the figure halfway. Once they were closer, the seller turned on a flashlight, shining its beam at Cody.

"<You speak Chinese?>" he asked.

"Not very well. Do you speak English?" Cody responded, blocking the light with his arm.

"Yes," replied the man in a perfect American accent.

He shined the flashlight toward the ground. Cody could see that he was an Asian man in his thirties.

"Good," the man smiled, "I'll give you the supplies when you show me the money."

The man motioned for Cody to follow him. The northeast part of downtown was a very dangerous area. Its shadows played tricks on the mind, amplifying paranoia. When Cody heard more than two pairs of footsteps, he knew that it wasn't his imagination. The man stopped and shined the flashlight back into Cody's eyes, blinding him from the glare. Instinctively, Cody knew he was surrounded by multiple people, but it was a mystery as to who they were.

"What's going on here?" he asked. "Who are you people?"

"Shut up and put your hands up," the man instructed.

Cody did as he was told. One of the figures, another

similarly aged Asian man, patted him down. Feeling Cody's wallet, he took it out and inspected it.

"I don't have much cash on me," Cody announced.

"We're not looking for your money," said the man holding the flashlight.

The man with Cody's wallet nodded his head to the man holding the flashlight. More flashlights turned on. Cody counted at least ten of them total.

They were wearing police uniforms.

The undercover officer read Cody his Miranda rights while another officer slapped a pair of handcuffs on him. Beads of sweat flowed down his forehead. He had never been treated like a criminal before. The police entered his information into their computer systems and ushered him into the back of a police car. He was soon hauled to the local HPD jailhouse. Never in his dreams would Cody imagine he'd have a mug shot. They took his front and side photos along with his fingerprints. It was a lot like the movies, except it wasn't as cute. He was then locked in a large cell alongside thirty or so other people.

"Hey!" called out an intimidating Caucasian man with tattoos covering his face. "Hey! I'm talking to you!"

Scared out of his mind, Cody continued looking down to avoid eye contact.

"What are you in for?!" asked the tattooed-face man.

He repeated the same question for awhile until he lost interest in Cody and pestered another. Cody tried to keep a positive mind, but he cursed himself for watching too many prison documentaries about inmate raping and the legend of jelly and syrup.

"Please, Jesus, please," he muttered in tears. "You said you'd be there if I needed you. You could show up in a basketball game. Why couldn't you show up now?"

"Jellyyyyy..." chimed in a skinny black man sitting across from Cody.

"Please, please, please, please," whispered Cody to his savior.

"Jellllyyyyyyyyyy..."

"Please, Jesus, please." He was noticeably audible now.

"Gonna put some jelly in my ass for ya!"

"Why aren't you showing up?!"

"Make ya eat it!"

"No! Aw, God, nooooo..."

The skinny black man cackled, "Ah, I'm just playin' wit' ya, ya dumb motherfucka!"

Forty-five minutes passed before Cody was allowed to make his only phone call. He didn't want to upset his parents. He didn't want to show this embarrassment to Daphne. He called the only person he could think of: Mindy.

"Bobbie, what's going on? How did the deal go? Did you get the stuff?"

"Mindy, I'm in jail," Cody said.

"Whaaaat?"

"Yeah, I'm in jail. Thanks to you. I told you I never wanted to do this shit."

"But how come you are in the jail?"

"You think I just walked in here on my own? They had an undercover cop."

"Undercover? I thought that was for drugs!"

"Oh, my God...You're so dumb."

"Hey, hey! I'm your best friend, okay? You do not call me a dummy."

"Why did I let you talk me into this?"

"Well, you did not complain when we made a lot of money, eh?"

"Whatever. I need bail."

"Bail? Bobbie, you know I'm not rich. Why don't I call your parents for you and have them bail you out?"

"No! Not only would they panic the hell out of

themselves, but the fact is, we're partners and you're partly responsible for this! You've got to come here with five thousand dollars and bail me the fuck out," demanded Cody.

"Stop saying those bad words."

"I'm sorry. Can you please just come over here and bail me? Please, I can't stay overnight with these thugs. There's minimal police protection. They're gonna..." Cody held back tears.

"They're gonna what, Bubble?"

"They're gonna...jelly..."

"Huh? Jelly?"

"Please, Mindy. Bail me. I'll pay you back."

"But I'm wearing my pajamas. My makeup is all washed off."

"Fucking A, Mindy. You're my best friend. You're going to let your best friend and business partner be stuck in a cell full of hardened criminals and thugs? They're going to rape me. They'll stick a dick inside of me, Mindy."

"Huh? Why would they do that? You are not a girl."

"Come on, I can't believe you have to even think about it! I gotta work tomorrow too! How am I going to tell our boss Rachel about this?"

"...five thousand dollars, right?"

"Yes."

"You must pay me back. Immediately. Write me a check."

"Of course."

"With a fifteen percent interest."

"What? You serious?"

"Yes."

"Come here and bail me out. And I'll write you a check for five thousand dollars. None of this interest nonsense. Are you my friend or not?"

"......fine. Give me an hour."

"An hour?!"

"Yes, an hour. I need to fix my hair and put on the makeup, man."

"What...ah..." Cody glanced back at the cell with the skinny black man chanting "jelly." "Okay, one hour. Please hurry."

As promised, Mindy arrived at the downtown jail house a little past midnight. Despite the abundant police presence, she felt a bit vulnerable with so many eyes looking at her from the waiting area. Catcalls and whistles were thrown her way while she posted bail at the counter. Not long afterwards, Cody came out, looking like a mess.

"Maaaaaaannnnnnnnnn," was all Mindy could utter.

Cody didn't respond. She handed him a ziplock bag filled with cookies.

"What's this?" asked Cody.

"Taiwanese coconut cookie," Mindy replied. "I knew you'd be hungry, Bobbie."

"You made it?" he asked, munching on two of them at once.

"Yeah. I made it......with money. HAHAHAHAHA!"

Cody glared at her with an odd look, "Where's your husband?"

"He's sleeping. He has to go to work tomorrow."

"Can't believe you came here alone, it's dangerous," Cody paused. "Um, did you...bring any water by any chance?"

"Oops."

They sat on a bench right outside of the police department. Cody stopped eating the cookies because they made him thirsty.

"Let's not do Mosaic Decor anymore," suggested Cody.

"Why not? We make money!"

"Yeah, but I do all the work."

"That's not true. I call them and I email them!"

"You weren't the one who just got arrested with some guy chanting 'jelly' at you for a few hours. It's not worth it."

"But, Bobbie, don't you like the freedom of owning your own business?"

Cody reflected on the pros and cons. "It does feel good to not answer to someone. We can set our own rates."

"And later hire more people. Then we don't have to do anything! Imagine, we go to vacation every week. People put money in our bank accounts! How lovely, huh?"

"You're already not doing anything, Mindy."

They both laughed.

"Okay. Fine, Bobbie. We will stop the Mosaic Decor. No more," Mindy replied. "But maybe someday, when you are more ready, you will have your own company, with employees, your own office and everything, right?"

Cody paused.

"You know," he smiled, "I never really thought about that before."

———

The business card was dark silver and slick, simplistic in design, yet strong in presence. It was no different from the hefty Asian man who had given it to her last month in Las Vegas. For at least once a day since then, Daphne had pulled it out of her purse and examined it. No one had challenged her to chase before. She was used to either the stumbling shy types or the overly zealous ones who exhausted their list of pick-up lines.

"Andrew Huynh," she read out loud.

It didn't sound anything like "Kyle Sawyer," the starting quarterback with the dreamy blond hair, broad shoulders and piercing blue eyes. Heck, she thought, it didn't even sound like "Cody Quan," nerdy and fun-to-talk-with web developer. Andrew could hide behind the nice suit and eloquent vocabulary, but Daphne knew a thug when she saw one. A CEO of a company that made identification tags? Yeah right, she thought, more like someone who probably stole car parts and sold jail-broke cell phones.

Her own cell phone suddenly vibrated.

It was Cody again; she had been ignoring him for weeks now. Even though they had seen one another in church, she had barely spoken to him. She didn't know why. It had all changed for her since meeting Andrew. When the vibrating finally stopped, Daphne glanced at the screen of her cell: Missed Call (18). It was part of a collection of unanswered replies. Deena: 22 missed calls. Ennis: 9 missed calls. Marion: 17 missed calls. Overall, there were around a hundred missed calls. Daphne didn't know what she was feeling. She had never felt this way before. Not even for Kyle. It certainly wasn't love.

She sighed and placed her phone down; but, just as soon, she found herself picking it back up again. As if in a trance, she started dialing the number on the card; she knew it by memory. With each ring that went by, Daphne fought herself to end the call.

"Hello?" answered the voice that had been replaying in her head.

".......hi," she finally replied.

"The girl from Vegas."

"Yes. Yes, it's me," Daphne nervously spoke. "I-I don't know why I'm calling."

"Join me for dinner."

"Right now? It's nine o'clock in the evening. I already

ate."

"You can watch me eat."

Daphne wanted to reply that she needed to be home in bed by ten o'clock. She wanted to tell him that she wasn't interested and that his response was more rude than humorous.

"Okay," she answered instead, "where are you?"

"IHOP."

"Are you alone?"

"Yes."

"Okay," Daphne paused, "tell me which one and I'll join you."

The IHOP he selected was a long ways from her townhouse, halfway across town. It was also particularly notorious for its loud customers and rude waitresses, seven days a week. For a presentable and sexy outfit, Daphne chose an olive green shirt matched with a tight pair of expensive jeans. She also put on makeup—not exactly knowing why, but did so anyway. Upon arrival, she saw him sitting at a center booth, busy in mid-conversation on his cell phone. It was unbelievable that this was the man who had been on her mind since Vegas.

"Yes...yeah...I see," Andrew continued on the phone. "Pete's been having cold feet. I don't know if he's cut out for this line of work. His friend's even worse...no...no, that's not the reason...his friend is the opposite problem. He's too daring...yeah...I suppose. Okay. Alright."

She ended up waiting for him for over thirty more minutes, listening to him chat about peculiar topics over the phone. When the conversation ended, he signaled for the check. None of the waitstaff had bothered to ask Daphne for an order.

"So," Andrew finally spoke to her, "what are we doing tonight?"

"I should go back home. I have to work tomorrow."

"Interesting. When do you work?"

"I have to get up at seven," she replied. "I arrive to

work at around eight-thirty."

"That's ten hours from now."

"Yeah."

"That's no problem. Here... " He pulled out two pills from his pocket and handed them to her. "These will keep you up."

"What are these?"

Andrew gave her a confused look.

"They're ex," he answered.

"These are ecstasy pills?!"

"Yeah. Good ones too. Let me know if you have friends that need any."

Daphne politely handed them back to Andrew.

"No, thanks," she replied.

"The milk drinking girl," he observed, "I see."

He kept silent while the waiter came back with his credit card. This was unfamiliar territory for Daphne. She expected attempts at small conversation, things like how her day went, what she believed in—details to woo her defenses down. When they had first met, he bought her a drink and shamelessly flirted with her. Tonight, however, he didn't even bother to ensure she had a glass of water. Some nerve, she thought.

"Well," he said getting up, "I'm heading out."

"Where are you going?"

"The Platinum Star."

"Isn't that a bad club? I hear bad things go on in there."

Andrew chuckled and shook his head. They both walked outside.

"You 'heard?'" he asked. "So that implies you've never been."

"No."

"Then how do you know it's 'bad?'" he asked, pulling out a cigarette and lighting it.

"I can't go with you. I have to go to work tomorrow."

He made a consistent stream of smoke come out from his lips.

"You work hard, but do you play hard?" he asked.

"I don't even know what that means."

With a cocky swagger, he unlocked his car via remote and left Daphne staring at him near the restaurant's entranceway. He rolled down the passenger side window while warming up his car.

"Choice is yours," he offered.

Daphne hesitated for a moment, clutching her crucifix necklace. She was seriously considering the devil's invite to hell. Satan was a hefty, unattractive, sleepless Vietnamese-American man who smelled like an ashtray and looked like vice. There were many reasons to fear him, but her soul would have none of it. She walked up to his passenger side door, opened it and, like Alice in Wonderland, descended into the rabbit hole.

"Let's roll," Andrew announced.

He set the stick shift to reverse, hightailing the car backwards from the parking lot. In a matter of seconds, the car was traveling over a 110 miles per hour on the beltway, prompting Daphne to hastily buckle her seat belt. The rush of air from the opened windows gave the superfluous speed its presence. Music pounding from amped-up audio systems—from radio station 104.1 KRBE, Daphne's favorite—gave the ride a melodramatic feel.

"Aren't you afraid of cops?" Daphne shouted in competition with the loud thumping sounds.

Andrew puffed on his cigarette and ignored her.

"I said 'Aren't you afraid of cops?'"she repeated.

"Cops?" He looked at her. "Cops are afraid of me."

Upon arriving and entering the notorious club, she discovered many of The Platinum Star's disreputable features were true. The people there were so different from her—inviting sin with their lascivious clothes and prurient movements. There was little class in them, so much that she couldn't relate and felt out of place.

"Go sit in the bar and ask for a man named Li'l Bis," Andrew instructed. "He should be the main bartender. Old black guy with an eye patch."

Daphne did what she was told and sat on one of the few vacant stools in the bar. She dreaded that her clothes would be reeking of the club's smell the next morning. None of the bartenders resembled anything like the description of Li'l Bis; they were all tough-looking girls who appeared hardened from years of no-nonsense bullshit. She was in mid-thought when suddenly a hand slipped underneath her and firmly squeezed the base of her buttocks. With a sudden reflex, Daphne infuriately confronted the culprit, bringing her face to face with a young weasel-looking Asian man.

"What say you and me pop some sugar, li'l mama?" he suggested.

She impulsively shoved him away, only to find that it encouraged him to try harder. Apparently, this was the culture of The Platinum Star.

"Come on, baby. You fine as hell!" the man insisted.

A firm hand placed itself atop his shoulders and moved him aside. The knight in shining armor was Andrew.

"Fuck!" The skinny man confronted him. "Nigga, ain't you believe you should think twice before layin' a hand on a nigga? This nigga spittin' game here, nigga!"

He invited Andrew to a challenge by flashing a pocket knife. Andrew smirked and revealed his Smith and Wesson Sigma SW40VE.

"Shit," the man replied, "this your lucky day, fat nigga."

He retreated back into the crowd, looking for another woman to harass.

"I couldn't find Li'l Bis," Daphne said.

"Must be his off night," Andrew shrugged, "or he's

taking a dump."

He ordered a shot of straight Grey Goose for Daphne. She wavered, but then gulped it down. Andrew held out two fingers to one of the bartenders, signifying two more shots.

"Andrew..." Daphne protested.

The bartender placed two more shots on the counter. Andrew gestured for her to drink another. Without hesitation this time, she drank it down. Four more shots came. Then another two. Then another three. By the time her brain could no longer count, she was led by her hand to an exclusive area behind the horde of dancers.

"Haha...hahaha!!!" The laughter was involuntarily coming out of Daphne.

Fragments of her reality defied any similitude for comprehension. She gathered that she was in a private room with men and women, most of whom were naked or partially naked. It was also odd that clones of her were in the room, eerily emulating her exact movements. Then a loud, unrecognizable roar of laughter came out from her. She realized she had been staring at her own reflections from the circumferential array of wall mirrors. By constantly blinking, she helped herself regain some partial awareness from her state of dizziness. Sex, she realized. The men and women were having sex. It was so difficult to think with fractions of information coming into her head. The white stuff on the glass tables—she shook her head—it was cocaine.

"Andrew, I don't...I don't want to do this..." muttered Daphne.

"I don't care."

He rolled up a hundred dollar bill and took a whiff of the drug. She saw herself doing the same. The shock to her nervous system quickly made her drop the rolled bill, sending her hands across the small heap of white powder. By the time she partially collected herself, she noticed her fingers smothered in cocaine, causing her to unleash a flurry of tears from guilt. Andrew gently slid a hand down her jeans and inserted a finger inside her. Without hesitation, his other hand began removing her shirt, all done without any request for permission.

It made Daphne feel like a whore.

"Please stop," she begged. "I don't know if I want to do this."

He motioned for one of the other girls to join. A blonde, Daphne was able to comprehend. Naked and kissing her too. It was all too fast, too sudden, too illogical. She was beginning to give in to the euphoria of meaningless, intuitive intercourse. Her morals meant nothing— her integrity an illusion. Perhaps, she feared, the main catalyst wasn't even the alcohol or drugs; it was a concealed desire within the depths of her soul.

"Andrew..." she repeated. This time her tone changed. She was no longer rejecting but inviting.

The exit sign visible from the corner of her eye no longer served as an appealing option. All she wanted to do now was swim in the madness that would set her free. She felt tongues encircling the circumference of her nipples until the arousal resulted in an out-of-body experience. Amid the iniquitous exchanges between male-to-female and female-to-female, Daphne felt the shame of hypocrisy bearing down on her conscience. It was hardly a week ago that she had taught a Sunday school class about virtue and chastity. Now she was a peddler of lies.

The sin had made her see that.

"Are...are you okay? Do you want to stop? You don't have to do this," assured the blonde girl.

That statement couldn't have been more wrong, thought Daphne. Nothing could substitute unrestrained freedom. Not the independence that compensated for a lost childhood from Beijing. Not the no-strings-attached conditions that Kyle Sawyer thought would be adequately befitting. And certainly not Jesus, who was more deadbeat than her own father. All she wanted for an imperfect life was the ideal boyfriend to fix it all. Someone who'd one day appear in her life and make it all worthwhile. Instead, Jesus couldn't even get that right. He gave her Cody Fucking Quan.

"YOU GAVE ME CODY FUCKING QUAN!" Daphne screamed.

"What?" asked the other girl, with a confused expression.

Daphne nudged her away and claimed Andrew as her own. Where her mind had seen scattered truths, the cocaine had clarified the truth. She closed her eyes and opened them again, knowing Jesus would be there. He was in the mirrors looking at her, looking at all the sinners engaging in a symphony of beautiful, emotion-filled sex and drugs. This kind of emancipation was what knowing Christ should have been. Too bad he never was. She climbed on Andrew, taking a long look at his body. He was fat, ugly and old; his naked body made him look like a whale. But she wanted so desperately to pleasure him in the dirtiest of ways. She belonged to him—an object without self-respect. A woman beneath a man.

"It's Daphne," she whispered, finally revealing her name to him. "My name is Daphne Lee."

———

All Jay Zheng ever wanted to know was the truth. He thought he would find it six years ago when he had run away from home. The sheltered Asian-American life wasn't for him; he needed to make mistakes. His parents, of course, had thought otherwise. Being perfect meant never making an error; being errorless meant living in protection. What it did was arouse his curiosity towards forbidden things—one of which was a drug habit. Running away from home had not taken much courage. It was an idea that had popped into his mind when he had first seen his favorite movie, *The Truman Show*. He had related to the concept of living in a bubble, unhappy with hiding in ignorance. It was tiring to hear everyone tease him about how innocent he was, so he did something about it.

And for a while he was right. The adventures of drug addiction and street hustling were a complete reversal from his pedestrian life. He learned more about reality in those two years than he had from the totality of his previous existence. In time, however, it introduced Jay to a different kind of misery. A worse kind. Drugs had enslaved him, forcing him to engage in embarrassing situations for every next high. The next destination was suicide; he couldn't imagine anything else.

Then he reunited with his old college friend Ennis, a devout Christian who brought him the teachings of Jesus. The concept was exemplary. It called for everyone to forgive themselves because Christ had forgiven them. Success was not measured financially but through living selflessly for others. The idea was inspirational; it simply asked for believers to give themselves entirely, unequivocally to Jesus.

The new purpose became his reality.

As a born-again Christian, he traded drug parties for soup drives, breaking comfort zones to explore his altruistic peak. The Word of Jesus was more addicting than the most potent heroin. It was a life that he had given himself into completely—a trust that transformed into dependency.

But then came the realization that some of his fellowship were keeping secrets. Some were homosexuals. Others were active fornicators. And then there were the child abusers. How could all this exist under the auspices of Fellowship Communion Baptist Church? Jay gave them the benefit of the doubt. He had to; his world would unravel.

It had crumbled earlier in the afternoon when he had sought a church official.

"Hello, Jay. Come. Sit down," the elder Reverend Han said. "I know what you're here to talk about."

It had been four weeks since Jay contemplated what he should do with Maple Washington's email. He figured it was better to give it to the senior church officials rather than local law enforcement. To his surprise, nothing happened. He wanted to know why.

"Jay," the stoic reverend began, "sometimes in order to do right, you have to make a bigger right. It forces hard decisions to be made. The kind of hard decisions for the long term, do you follow me?"

He paused and cleared his throat before continuing.

"Pastor Washington may have done a sin, but he is a good pastor. Because of him, church attendance has doubled and donations have tripled! We were very hesitant to bring in a black group, but we realize now that our black membership is much more generous than our Chinese membership. To cut off this pastor is to cut off our budget. Look at how many new members we are able to bring in now because of our wealthy status! Nobody wanted to come to a low-financed church before. But now... now we are growing! Pastor Washington is God's blessing. Sometimes God wants us to turn a blind eye upon the imperfections of His gifts because there's a bigger gift."

Satisfied with his own answer, the reverend proceeded to ask if Jay had sent the video to anyone else.

"Only you, Reverend Ping and Pastor Lu," he replied.

"Good. That's good," murmured Reverend Han. "I want you to do one more favor for me. Log on to your Gmail account here on my computer and delete the email. For good."

After Jay did what he was told, the reverend clasped his hands together and smiled.

"Everything will be alright," smiled the reverend. "You'll see. It was just an overreaction on Maple's part."

Jay left the office unsatisfied. It was now clear to him that the church was a business. A crooked one at that, thought

Jay. A haven for liars and crooks who hid behind the name of God and the good intentions of people—a green light for their character flaws.

Now that his reason for clean living had ceased, he set out to do the one thing he had never done: he wanted to get laid. It was funny, he realized. There was never an opportunity or desire to have intercourse before. Until tonight, sex had been such a sacred thing. His parents forbade it, his drug habits took priority over it, and his church taught him to save it for marriage. None of that mattered anymore; he decided he might as well experience it. It was interesting how the trip from his home to the district with the neon-lit homes was just twenty minutes away. There were so many of them, in fact, that he drove past twice trying to make a decision. Each of the signs looked so similar: Jade Spa, Eternal Massage, Happy Paradise...there were fifteen to twenty in one block alone. Jay finally decided on a smaller one, a place called Oriental Endings.

Upon arrival, he took a deep breath and let the remaining nervousness remove itself from his body. He found the front door was a bit of an enigma for a first-timer. It was sealed by an iron gate with a security camera tracking him from the top. The doorbell was concealed rather astutely, disguised as a plastic flower petal on the wall. Seconds after he had rung it, a pretty Thai girl in a bikini opened the door. She was beyond gorgeous, thought Jay, so attractive that he didn't feel worthy of her friendliness. That opinion quickly explicated when a line of other pretty young Asian women marched in front of him inside the massage parlor.

"You can choose as many as you want. Each for a hundred and sixty dollars an hour," informed the smiling Thai girl.

Jay took his time to decide. He eyed each girl carefully. Some of the girls giggled, some looked tired and some looked angry. He eventually decided on who he thought was the friendliest-looking girl.

"I'll take her," he replied.

She led him to a private massage room where he was asked to pay first. After taking his money, the girl left him alone to remove his clothes. Then he wrapped a towel around his private parts and waited. He silently laughed at all the sexually suggestive decorations; there were lava lamps, naked figurines, displayed champagne bottles, Kenny G CDs. All of these served as entertaining distractions until the sound of the door opening interrupted his thoughts. The girl he had chosen signaled for him.

"Please, come with me," she smiled. "What is your name, sir?"

"Jay, what's yours?" he said, walking around the spa's hallways with both hands holding his towel.

"Flower."

"That's a pretty name."

"Thank you."

On their way to the shower rooms, they passed by other men and giggling spa girls, who were venturing both directions of the hallway. It was disturbing that most of the men looked like they were likely married with children; a majority of them were twice the ages of the young women. Flower made sure Jay was comfortable as he lay across the wet plastic shower bed before bathing him with a gentle stream of water and her soft fingers. Her fingernails teased his buttocks as she applied soap and rubbed his genitals clean. Throughout the shower, she retained a plastered smile, which made Jay wonder how she could maintain it in a job like this.

"Where are you from?" asked Jay.

"I am from Thailand," she answered. "What about you?"

"I was born and raised here in Houston."

"But you are Chinese or Korean or what?"

"My parents are from China."

"Oh. Chinese customers usually do not tip so well. Will you tip me well?"

"Of course," smiled Jay, "pretty girl like you deserves it."

"Thank you! Thank you!"

After the table shower, they retraced their steps back from the same hallway and returned to their private room. This time instrumental covers of classic love songs were playing in the background. Jay enjoyed himself while lying face down in the sensual bed, relishing the oil rubdown Flower gave him. He was impressed with the vigorous strength she was able to muster from her tiny body. When she felt that he was at ease, she dipped her body closer, pressing her perky breasts across his back. This triggered a natural erection from Jay, which she encouraged by playing with his genitals in an alternating pattern between her left and right hands. Knowing he was ready, she gently kissed his ear and asked him to turn over.

"I know what you want. I know why you really came here," she whispered.

Using her mouth, she applied a condom on him with a skill that dazzled Jay with its precision as much as it had aroused him. The girl closed her eyes, engaging in her usual motions of impersonal intercourse. There was a rehashing of the same sounds and grunts she had memorized over the years of her occupation. It distracted and unnerved Jay, knowing sex was just another fabricated gratification in his life.

"Oh, baby, come on, come on. Please cum. Oh yeah, you're the best, so good," she chanted emotionlessly. It was in the tone of a parent hurrying a child to eat vegetables.

He made the most of it by focusing on her bouncing breasts. It helped when he dismissed the higher functions of his brain and delved into its primitive urges to dominate and replicate. Soon enough, in one explosive, calming conclusion, Jay enjoyed the biological benefits of emancipating his urge. Flower's acting immediately ended. She quickly slipped into her nightgown and flushed the condom down the bathroom toilet.

"Do you still want some more massage? You have ten minutes left," she informed.

"No, it's okay," Jay replied. "Hey, what's your real name?"

"I...cannot tell you."

"That's alright. Why do you do this job? Do you like it?"

Flower's expression changed to a serious one.

"Of course, I don't like it. No girl here like it. All we do is fuck, fuck, fuck. We have no choice."

She spent the remaining time giving him a solid back massage until a buzzer sounded.

"Okay, put on your clothes. It's time to go," instructed Flower.

Her sudden impersonal demeanor only added to Jay's rediscovered cynicism. The door slammed shut behind him immediately after he had left the property. He knew he would never enter through it again. Still, he thought, there was plenty of time left before his planned objective for the evening. He decided not to rush it, sitting outside the spa's parking lot and enjoying the cloudless night sky. It was a shame that he knew God existed, only to realize the guy was a jerk. How could an omnipresent being so sagacious leave the world in such an imperfect state? He could create millions of stars, yet was incapable of preventing war and poverty. If Jay hadn't given up so dispiritedly, he might have felt a tinge of confounding disappointment. Not anymore. Instead, he basked in the sign's neon glow, enjoying its uniquely soothing comfort.

He would sit there for a few hours.

Just around midnight, Jay arrived in front of his church, carrying a large tote bag. Despite its fancy new security systems, it was no sweat for him to breach the building. He did feel a tinge of rust from his breaking and entering days, but it was mere child's play, nonetheless. Besides, he wondered, how much faith did the congregation really have if it depended on security systems anyway?

Using a combination of hairpins, a small knife and a screwdriver, he was able to pick the locks, making his way into the church. Things felt different at night. Without its crowds and lighting, Fellowship Communion Baptist Church lost its mystique. Jay couldn't resist walking up to the podium, imagining what it would feel like to preach on a Sunday morning. There was a powerful presence to it, he felt, no doubt about that. Unfortunately, the feeling wasn't spiritual; it was authoritative. With such a rush of power, Jay realized, it was inevitable that even the best-intentioned pastors would eventually turn to corruption.

When he finally had enough of the podium, he decided it was time to accomplish his primary mission. He made his way toward several of the Bible study rooms, observing their ceiling fans and optimal visibility from the entrance. He found just the

one in the children's day care center, which offered the closest
distance between its own doorway and the front. There, he
collected the teacher's stool and calculated weight comparisons.
It was perfect, he determined, though he regretted it would be
done in the room where he once substituted for Sunday school.
He reminisced about it as being one of his more happier
memories, teaching Noah's ark to eager children who held on to
every word he said. One day they'll know it was a lie; he wished
he could be there to apologize.

But he wouldn't.

Jay plopped down his tote bag and removed a laptop
and rope from it. While waiting for the computer to load, he
wasted no time in contriving a perfect noose from the rope. It
was made from good material, admired Jay—very sturdy and
capable of doing its job. Turning his attention back to the
laptop, Jay entered the wi-fi codes of the church and logged
into his email account. Though Reverend Han had asked him to
delete the email, he had never asked Jay if he had saved it on his
hard drive. Composing a long and detailed email about what
happened to Maple and his grievances with the church, he felt
proud to contribute one last act of greater good before expiring
from the world. He attached Maple's video and retrieved the
email contacts from the church's directory. Jay reviewed it one
final time, took a deep breath and clicked Send All.

Now for the second part.

He took out a handwritten letter from his pocket,
placing it underneath the stool. Then, without hesitation, he
made his way on top of the stool and adjusted the rope and
noose accordingly for a good hang. Before his departure,
however, he waited for the figure to walk into the room. He
knew Jesus would come; he wanted the Messiah to see this.
They looked at one another in silence, both knowing it would
not be stopped. Without breaking eye contact, Jay kicked the
stool out of the way, allowing gravity to do its job. Jesus stood
and watched as the body became lifeless, hanging like a puppet
on a broken string.

CHAPTER 12: THE END

The first screams were heard at approximately seven-thirty in the morning. They came from a church member who was in charge of xeroxing the service programs. The second person to scream was one of the choir women. She had come over to the day care room only because she had heard the previous woman scream. Neither of the pastors had arrived yet. Jay's lifeless body remained slowly twirling from the rope—a haunting visage that was covered by a partially closed door until emergency workers arrived.

"Did you know how the deceased person came in?" asked the policeman.

"N...no..." stammered the crying Xerox lady.

"When was the last time you had interaction with this individual?"

"I'm not...sure...I...I even recognize..."

"What's going on here?" chimed in Pastor Lu, who had just arrived.

"Sir, who are you?" asked the officer.

"I'm the pastor of this church!" he declared. "Members were calling me, telling me what had happened! I came as fast as possible!"

The officer led the pastor to a quieter outdoors area to question him. The abundance of police cars and crime scene tape quickly drew the curiosity of the locals. Through the windy mid-November weather they looked onward, clutching their coats in a struggle to observe what had happened. Rumor had it that someone was murdered. Another suggested an armed lunatic was on a shooting spree. By the time Cody had arrived, it was a challenge to separate truth from fiction.

"Oh, Lord, I saw...that body too..." cried one of the black women he often had seen there.

"What's going on? I heard the word 'body.' Did someone die?" asked
Cody.

"Yeah, they found Jay's body," Felix softly replied. "He committed suicide."

"Inside of the church?!"

Felix nodded, "There...there was a note."

"A note?"

"Cody, did you check your emails this morning?"

"No, but what did the note say?"

"It said for us to check our emails."

Cody caught sight of a person heading in their direction. It was Marco, boiling with anger as he charged through the crowd.

"TELL ME IT'S A LIE!" he ordered Felix.

"What's a lie?" Felix questioned.

"THE EMAIL JAY WROTE!"

"What? Calm down, man!"

He shoved Felix down to the ground, prompting others to hold and restrain him.

"Dude, what are you mad about?!" asked Felix.

"YOU'RE A FAGGOT. A HOMOSEXUAL! JAY SAW YOU INAPPROPRIATELY KISSING LUKE!" Marco shouted.

Felix was at a loss for words.

"SO IT'S TRUE?!" pushed Marco.

"Yes, it's true," spoke another voice. It was Luke.

"Oh, my gosh," gasped one of the church members.

"The pastor's son..." commented another.

Luke helped Felix up.

"Felix and I," Luke declared, "are lovers."

Hearing that detail sent Marco into a bolt of rage. He

found the strength to free himself, charging at Luke like a bull.

"Marco, no!" screamed Ennis, tackling Marco in mid-charge.

"THEY'RE GOING TO HELL! BOTH OF THEM! I'M SERIOUS!" he screamed.

Several police officers intervened, preventing further attack. Marco was shaking so hard he turned red. Several church members glared at Luke and Felix, uncertain of their trust in them after their deception.

"Look, everyone!" interrupted Marion.

A collective gasp erupted as the covered body of Jay Zhang was seen being carted off into an ambulance.

"It's...oh, my Lord...it's Jay's body," muttered Henry.

"Hey, has anyone seen Pastor Washington?" interrupted one of the church members.

"Didn't you read the email sent by that boy?" replied another.

"No, what happened?"

"He was beating Maple."

"For real?"

"It was caught on tape. Figured it was recorded by the girl herself."

Back in Quentin Washington's home, the guilty pastor looked into his own red eyes in the mirror and acknowledged his shame. The email from Jay had reached him that morning just as it had reached the others, including the news of Jay's self-demise. Washington's heart knew the consequences of his mistakes weren't premeditated, but nevertheless his ungodly decisions were still influential in what resulted. The pastor knew he was partially to blame for the disillusions that caused the young man to take his own life. He figured there was only one remaining thing left to do now before police arrived. The Bible commanded him to make peace; it was time to give a heartfelt apology to his daughter. Maple had barricaded herself in her room the whole morning, perhaps in fear of his retribution. He wanted to make sure she knew he had no such intention. He struggled with the words he needed to say, but he found them once he approached the front of her locked door.

"Daddy's probably going to get into a lot of trouble for

this. But I just want you to know," Washington said in tears, "that I love you, Maple. And I'm sorry for what I did."

"YOU'RE SORRY THAT YOU GOT CAUGHT!" Maple screamed.

"One day, I'll hope you'll forgive me."

It was the last time most of the members from Fellowship Communion Baptist Church would hear from the pastor. It wasn't too long before the rumor mill also got a hold of the other leaders withholding evidence. Both Chinese and black members left the church and joined other congregations. At the height of its short-lived popularity, Fellowship Communion Baptist Church had grown to 253 members. By the end of the week following Jay's death, the membership was down to 35. The mid-sized church soon closed until further notice.

————————

A week after Jay's death, it was Skinny Grandma's funeral. The Buddhist chants stretched into long monotonous sessions—sounds not designed for audio gratification but for clear passageways of the soul. Every now and then, there would be a chime, a slight pause, and the same repeat of jumbled words foreign to Cody's ears. These were his first impressions of his grandmother's funeral, contrasting it between today and Jay's Christian funeral from a day before. As much as one can "enjoy" a funeral, he found the Christian customs more positive. The usually dry Pastor Lu gave a surprisingly ardent sermon about seeing rare blessings in dark times. It was ironic how they celebrated more of Jay's life in death than in person; yet it was an honorable celebration, nonetheless.

Not so with Skinny Grandma's Buddhist funeral.

There was a deliberate gloom to it as if sadness and suffering pleased the deceased. A certain power and allure resulted from its sturdy mystique. After awhile, all of its participants fell into a spell, chanting along with the monks. Cody momentarily resisted the hypnotizing effect by focusing on the others who were there. Duke stood statue-like, impenetrable but visibly saddened. His grandfather was lost in memory, with each tear a remembrance of times past. Most notable was the melodrama coming from his aunts and father who treated the funeral like it was a stage audition.

"<Shout louder and cry louder>," his father encouraged him. "<We want her spirit to know how upset we are. It'll make her take pity on us and bring good luck. More money. A new car. Your grandmother has the power to bless us with such things now, son!>"

The eulogy after the chant session gave the funeral a momentary resemblance of normalcy. One of Cody's more charismatic uncles delivered a heartfelt speech, though Duke's stoic translation rendered it colorless. The uncle mostly stammered, ultimately repeating his only point four times more than necessary.

"<No matter how much we love life and the people in it>," he said for a final time, "<in the end, we all must part ways.>"

Afterwards, the funeral participants gathered in line, paired through individual families. They were each given some incense and a rose—the former for bowing and placing in the thurible, the latter for the open casket. Every now and then the line stalled because a relative had fainted or had trouble moving on. Cody was near the end of the line. When it was his turn, he barely made more than a passing glance at his grandmother's body. He felt it was better to deal with his emotions this way. After all, he thought, the body was nothing more than a lifeless husk whose omnipresent soul anticipated its next destination. He made a halfhearted bow of respect to the body and dropped his rose in, watching it land closely to her crossed arms.

"Goodbye, mah mah," he muttered.

By design, the last person in line was Cody's

grandfather. The elderly Quan stood and stared at the casket for what seemed like an eternity. He stared with a concentrated focus, seemingly to bid his final farewell telepathically. It was a gesture far more genuine and powerful than the showy pantomimes that promulgated the funeral. Then, with a calm release from his fingertips, the last rose was gently dropped and landed near her heart. With that done, the funeral director took over and closed the casket.

Cody, the last male heir, was given the task of holding his grandmother's portrait during the walk to the incinerator room. The rest of the family followed with the casket in tow, carried by Duke, Cody's father and two of his uncles. At first, Cody thought the constant chills up and down his body came from the monks' chanting in front of him. He then realized the cold feeling was literal; the sections away from the chapel had piercingly low temperatures.

It was enough to let his guard down, allowing sentiment to ride with him the rest of the way. He owed his grandmother that much. They were all good memories, even the bad ones. Sometimes they were simple like dribbling a basketball in the parking lot. Others were humorous, like the childhood pranks Duke and Cody had pulled on the old woman. These fragments of yesterday collided together in a place that was forever accessible. It was where Cody wanted to be after he died—a better afterlife than the exclusive heaven of Christian lore. Jesus, he thought, could have Marco, Pastor Washington, Daphne and Deena. Let those hypocrites congregate inside of their own corner of eternity. For him, the choice was simple: He wanted to reside in unconditional love.

The incinerator room could only be described as a decoration-less area that made no apologies for its purpose. It was located apart from the main building, residing in a warehouse that also held extra furniture and supplies. At the end of the room was the incinerator itself. It was a rusty metallic furnace attached to a conveyor belt where the casket would be placed and later dropped. While the four casket holders prepared the positioning of the coffin for the final fallout, the monks maximized the volume and speed of their chanting. The service had arrived to its dramatic conclusion where nary a dry eye remained. As they watched the casket slide into the idle incinerator, Cody stood next to his grandfather and grasped his arm as a show of support. The funeral director led Cody's father to the power button, indicating it was time to turn the furnace on. With a deep breath and wobbly knees, Mr. Quan closed his eyes and quickly pressed it.

In a moment of efficiency devoid of hesitation—one in which only a machine could provide—the incinerator wasted no time coming to life.

The raw reality of hearing the strong flames engulf Skinny Grandma's body was enough to send Cody's heart fainting. He repeatedly uttered Jesus' name as a means for comfort, partially praying for illogical wishes like turning back time or realizing it was a dream. Eventually, the family members left the incinerator room one after the other. Cody and his grandfather were the last to go.

Once outside, he saw distant relatives he hadn't visited with since childhood. Most of them had crossed into the married-with-children life, finding him difficult to relate to. Duke, however, was showered with congratulations as he flaunted his new girlfriend, Annebelle, around. He presented himself with a dignified pose, absorbing their praises as though they belonged to him. Seeing his cousin alone, Ace offered conversation.

"<Hey, ehh, cousin Cody, ehh, sorry about your grandmother>," said Ace.

"It's okay, man," waved off Cody. "Life goes on. Thanks for coming. I know this isn't your side of the family, but I appreciate it anyway."

"<Do you, ehh, want some time alone? Eh, can I pray for something?>"

"Trust me, the last thing I want to do is pray."

"<Ehh, okay. I'm just checking. Eeh, cousin Cody, may I ask you a small question?>"

"Yeah?"

"<I heard that someone died in your church and then it closed. Do you want to go to mine?>" offered Ace.

"No, thanks," answered Cody, "I'm done with churches."

"Yo, look this way you li'l bitch!" demanded Danny.

The tiger glared at him, hoping its stare would be ample warning. Danny ignored it and continued taunting.

It was his way of staving off boredom on a cool December morning, where he and Pete were early for a drug meeting at the Houston Zoo. A zoo employee on Piranha's payroll had let them in, leading them to the tiger exhibit where they would meet Andrew. The two had an idea about why they were summoned here. Danny had been attracting attention with his lavish drug parties—ones where he often gave away free cocaine. Pete repeatedly warned his young Cambodian friend about his bold attitude, but it only strengthened Danny's resolve.

"Damn, nigga," cautioned Pete, "stop pissin' that tiger off. We in trouble enough as it is."

"Why you all scared of them niggas, bra?" Danny countered. "You knew they just gonna tell us to lay back!"

"Morning, gentlemen," interrupted a voice. Andrew and his associate had just arrived on the scene. As usual, he was dressed in nice business attire. Both held a cup of coffee.

"Heh," snarled Danny, "I see you tryin' to get all Scarface on us with this tiger. Trying to make you look like a bad muthafuck. Ain't gonna work, my nigga."

Andrew smirked, staring at his coffee.

"You gotta excuse Danny," intervened Pete. "He been a bit high these couple of days, heard?"

"Oh, yeah," chuckled Andrew, "I heard."

"For the real tho'," insisted Danny, "y'all ain't our mommy and daddy. We grown ass niggas. We done deal how we done deal, y'all feel me?"

Andrew calmly finished his coffee and responded, "You know what's the problem with getting cookies from the jar?"

"What, this Pillsbury doughboy the Riddler now?" laughed Danny.

"One forgets to leave tips," replied Andrew. "I thought

I taught you both better than that. Throwing parties, giving away free shit."

"Oh, so what now, nigga, you gonna shoot us hea in th' zoo?" commented Danny. "You outta ya damn mind!"

The high he was under made Danny dangerously braver than he had reason to be, strutting around the edge of the exhibit.

"Go ahead an' shoot me then, nigga!" he continued. "I'm bulletproof, fool!"

Andrew's associate took out a gun and pointed it at Pete instead.

"Ay ay ay!" protested Pete, "what you pointin' that at me fo'? I ain't start shit! Them parties weren't my idea, nigga!"

The associate continued holding Pete at gunpoint while walking towards him. He then surprised Pete by pulling out a pair of scissors.

"Hahaha! He gonna cut off your li'l dick, man!" Danny laughed.

Pete heard the scissors trimming off pieces of his hair. The associate gathered samples of it until he had the small quantity that he needed.

"Dang, yo, I was gonna cut my hair anyway!" grinned Pete. "I do it once every Tuesday. What's going on here?"

The associate nodded to Andrew, who took out his own gun and pointed it at Danny.

"Nigga, what the hell is going on?!" Danny asked.

Pieces of Pete's hair were sprinkled over Danny's clothes. It was enough to discourage suspicion. A fifth person joined them—a police officer.

"Meet one of HPD's finest on our payroll," introduced Andrew. "He's going to serve witness to Pete murdering you."

"Huh? You clownin' or what, you fat motherfucka?" Danny taunted.

With a sudden motion, the associate grabbed Danny, flinging him into the tiger's den. The fall injured the young Cambodian's leg. He watched helplessly as the tiger approached him.

"Ah shit, nigga! Ah damn, nigga!" screamed the Cambodian youth.

Pete flinched in horror as he heard inhuman screams of agony and pain. The sounds of bones crunching and blood squirting ensured an inerasable memory.

Then there was silence.

"Officer," Andrew ordered, pointing at Pete, "arrest this man."

The setup had begun. Pete would take the rap and the corrupted officer would make the paperwork legit. There wasn't any use for squealing either; Piranha had deep reaches into Pete's family.

"If you stay low and keep silent, we'll get you out in about five to seven years. Even at first-degree," winked Andrew. "We have friends in high places."

He departed with his associate, leaving the officer to report on the crime.

———

Cody lay awake in the middle of the night while his home phone was left ringing. He knew who it was, but he was too angry to answer her. After a long week that spanned through two funerals, he was also too emotionally exhausted to care. When the ringing stopped, the calling pattern alternated to his cell phone. They were guilt calls from Daphne, he knew. Ever since her surprising infatuation with her new "friend" Andrew, she had forgotten anyone else existed. He was tired of her selfish nature; the only thing she was entitled to was his cold shoulder. She had intentionally ignored his calls, and to top it all off, she had forgotten his twenty-eighth birthday. The least she could do, thought Cody, was stick with her self-centeredness and leave him alone. When the calls continued coming an hour afterwards, her persistency finally won out over his stubbornness.

"Hi," he answered.

"Hi, Cody. Happy birthday," said Daphne in her

familiar passive voice.

"Hey."

"Why.......haven't you been returning my phone calls?"

"..."

"Cody?"

"I thought you slept before ten o'clock on Mondays."

"It's a winter holiday, Cody."

"Okay. Well, thanks for remembering."

"Why would I forget? We're friends, remember?"

"Yeah? Friends who ignore each other's calls now."

"You're the one who've stopped picking up. I've called you and called you."

"And who was ignoring who between September and November?"

"That's different, Cody. I got so much to share with you."

"About your new boyfriend, I'm sure. I've heard the rumors, Daphne."

"He's not my boyfriend. He's just my friend."

"Hah!...ha....ehhhh.......Jesus Christ," Cody said.

"I don't know what's wrong with me these days, Cody. I miss you so much. I miss our friendship. Do you wanna have some coffee with me sometime? Please?"

"You're begging me now? That's fucking rich."

"I just don't understand why you're so mad. I don't want you to hate me, Cody."

"I don't hate you. I just don't give a damn anymore."

"..."

"It's liberating."

"Cody, I need to tell you about my...friend Andrew. I don't know what he does."

"Well, where's your so-called friend now?"

"That's the thing. He constantly comes and goes. He's so mysterious. I don't know what's wrong with me, Cody. Tell me what's wrong with me, please?"

"You don't know what he does?"

"He says he sells I.D. tags, but...okay, like once he went to the zoo in the early morning. And he told me it was for I.D.'s. But who does that? He's already lied to me about so many things. About his age, his motives, everything. And the friends he has are so suspect. They just play poker all the time and smoke."

"And you go with him to these poker games?"

"Yes, Cody. I would stay with him until sunrise. I couldn't go to work so I quit my job. I don't know what to do with my friend Andrew."

"Daphne, what do you see in this guy?"

"What?"

"You're obviously in love with him. What do you see in him?"

"I'm not in love with him!" giggled Daphne.

"..."

"I mean, he's a leader. He's got the nicest dog in the world. He cooks for me—"

"I cook for you too."

"Yeah, but I mean, he also cooks for his dog!"

"......are you on crack?"

"A little," laughed Daphne, "I'm just kidding! That was a joke, Cody. Oh, I missed talking with you so much. Andrew doesn't talk much."

"You heard what happened to the church, right?"

"I think so. Isn't it time for the Christmas bake sale?"

"Daphne, Pastor Washington was caught abusing Maple. She told Jay, who in return told church officials, who tried to bury it, and then he goes and hangs himself."

"Oh? Is Jay okay?"

"He's dead, Daphne! While you were on your little rendezvous with your 'friend' Andrew, shit went down. Your little friends from church had been worried sick about you. Who the fuck is this Andrew guy? Why is he so important to you that you abandoned your friends, your job and even your own dreams?"

"I...I don't know. I just...it's just the way he makes me feel, I guess. You know just the other day he took me out to the gun range. He was SO good with his gun. He taught me how to fire. I loved the gun range! But he also does gentle things like golf too. Every day is a new experience with him!" Daphne smiled.

"Jay died. Do you...understand that?" Cody repeated. "And our friendship died as well."

"Of course, I'm shocked that Jay died. Cody, I miss you. Can you buy some of my time shares? It would help pay rent. Andrew borrowed money from me, but he'll pay me back soon."

"You don't even sound like you anymore. It's like I'm talking to a different person. A person who's lost it."

"Maybe you can get me into your home decor business."

"So this is who you really are. That whole Christian persona was just bullshit. This is you. The real you. I gotta say I'm not impressed, Daphne."

"Are you going to abandon me now? We're friends, Cody. You're not supposed to abandon me."

"I was a friend who had feelings for you. I was a friend to you because it was the only way to get you to talk with me. And now you just want to be friends because you're dating a suspect guy and you quit your damn job and you want money from me, is that it?"

"No, of course not—"

"I love you, Daphne Lee."

"You're...you're so silly, Cody," giggled Daphne.

A door opening could be heard. A dog barked.

"Why do I hear a dog barking?" asked Cody.

"He's back! I'll call you later, okay?"

"You live with him now?! Is that his dog?"

"Hey, do you want to go on a ski trip with my friend Andrew and I?"

"Why the fuck would I want to go on a ski trip with you and that guy together?"

"Who's that?" Andrew said in the background.

"Just a friend," replied Daphne, "hey, I made you some dinner. It's on the kitchen table."

Daphne returned to her phone conversation with Cody.

"Sorry about that. Where were we?" she asked. "Hello? Cody, are you there?"

Cody had hung up.

—————

"January 9, 2006. Monday.

I don't know how to start this blog. I suppose for my first entry I'll summarize my day back at work. Rachel Higgins, my supervisor, came to me with a smile. Usually when she smiles, that signifies bad news. Sure enough, they've successfully assigned a new supervisor to me. It's that asshole from the I.T. department. Forgot his name at the moment. But that was a move to make my life hell. Also, Mindy stopped interning and she'll focus full-time on her doctorate. We'll still talk, but probably not on a day-to-day basis.

First day alone sucked. Not much to look forward to anymore. I used to be so excited when I thought God was in my life. I can't say I don't believe in the existence of God, but I don't believe I'm cared for. Ennis lied to me. He said if I gave my heart up to Jesus, better things would happen. All I saw was hypocrisy. It isn't so much with Jay dying or Washington beating up his kid. It wasn't just Daphne falling for a bad guy or Zoey leaving the church or basketball games erupting in violence. It wasn't Jesus miraculously healing my grandmother only to kill her just as quickly. It wasn't any one thing among many things...

...it was just all of those things.

Today, I went to the bathroom and took off my crucifix. Jesus came in and looked at me. He always seems to show up when it doesn't matter or whenever it is too late. Jesus gives me the impression that he's a deadbeat. He might as well wear a wife-beater. Anyway, I looked at him and then I dropped the crucifix into the toilet. I told him to talk to me and give me something, anything, that would stop me from flushing it down into the sewer. If he had just said something meaningful, anything meaningful, I would have dipped my hands into that piss-soaked dump bucket and picked it back up. But he just said nothing and looked on. So I flushed the crucifix down the toilet. Then I closed my eyes, opened them, and Jesus was gone.

I don't know why I decided to make my first entry about my day. I figured it probably contained some of the most important things that mattered to me. It feels good to finally write about them. Free from having to worry about God's wrath. I quit being a Christian. I don't know who'll care to find this blog and read it. But hopefully some day, someone out there can find my words relatable. For now, I'm just putting my thoughts down as therapy.

Well, here's to a life of monotony. When it's all said and done, I'm back to square one again."

- From the first journal entry of Cody Quan.

END OF ACT I

ACKNOWLEDGEMENTS

I've always told my father that I'm supposed to achieve more than him and my mother. Without their help and hard work, I wouldn't have had the opportunities to exceed them. That's the sign of progression and the ultimate way of rewarding a previous generation's lifetime of dedication and sacrifice. I will never forget that they were the ones who brought me here and they were the ones who stuck with me during a struggling time in my life. The existence of this book shall long outlive us and future generations of the Leung family. By showing my parents proper recognition here, their loving and unselfishness will hopefully be immortalized. I know it's not enough to repay them as wonderful parents, but it's a start. I would also like to thank a very good friend in Nori Choy who encouraged and pushed me to start and finish this book. Her constant feedback and early grammar fixing made writing this book very enjoyable. To my editor, Ron Lewis, I thank him for his professionalism and hard work; like all great editors, he's made me look smarter than I really am. Finally, I'd like to give a special appreciation to all the ones who helped in the marketing of the first act of Cody Quan.

PLEASE LIKE US ON FACEBOOK:

www.facebook.com/louisleungauthor

PLEASE FOLLOW US ON TWITTER:

@louisleungautho

WEBSITE:
http://www.louisleungauthor.com